DREAM HOUSE

Maltilda explored the house that Arden offered her. In the dressing room she found clothes for every occasion, all the first style of fashion, all in colors that would set off her creamy skin and fiery hair. Dashing bonnets, gloves of softest kid, slippers of gold and colored satin peeked out at her.

Then she entered the bedroom. There were mirrors in the most inconceivable places. And a vast, gold-curtained bed.

Matilda stared at the bed. She could almost see Arden in it, cradling her in his strong arms. He would be gentle, that she knew. He would be passionate.

And Matilda knew she must escape this house . . . while she could . . . *if* she could . . .

MARGARET WESTHAVEN is a native Oregonian. She is married and has a young son.

SIGNET REGENCY ROMANCE
COMING IN APRIL 1991

Carla Kelly
Libby's London Merchant

Melinda McRae
The Duke's Daughter

Gayle Buck
Mutual Consent

BY THE EDITORS OF CONSUMER GUIDE®

WALK
INTO
SHAPE

Consultant: **Peggy Norwood Keating, M.A.**

D1560208

Consultant: **Peggy Norwood Keating, M.A.,** is an exercise physiologist and serves as Fitness Director for the Duke University Diet and Fitness Center. She is a member of and is certified by the American College of Sports Medicine and the National Strength and Conditioning Association.

Contributing Writer: **Rebecca Hughes**

Illustrations: **Susan Spellman**

Cover Photo: **Caroline Wood/International Stock**

CONTENTS

Introduction: From Here to There 5

These days, walking is more than just getting from one place to another—and here's why.

Chapter 1: Walking into Fitness 11

If you're tired of exercise that hurts and diets that don't work, try walking—and discover a healthier, fitter you.

Chapter 2: Walking for the Health of It 30

A regular walking program can help fight off heart disease and make you feel younger than your years.

Chapter 3: Leave the Blahs Behind 42

Got the blues? A walking program can help relieve depression, anxiety, and daily tension.

Chapter 4: Getting Ready to Go 52

Here's how to check out your health and diet *before* you begin your exercise program.

Chapter 5: Freestyle Fitness Walking 69

Developed by Consumer Guide®, these walking programs allow you to progress at your own pace.

Chapter 6: Racewalking 81

Are you looking to pick up the pace? If you like challenge and competition, racewalking may be just your speed.

Chapter 7: Hiking 93

Hiking is a great way to get more out of your walking program. Here's how to hit the trail safely.

Chapter 8: Stretches and Strengtheners 105

No fitness program is complete without warmups, cooldowns, stretches, and strengtheners.

Chapter 9: Coping with Pain 117

Here's how to deal with any pain or discomfort you may encounter on the walking path.

Chapter 10: Walk, Weather or Not 141

You'll probably want to walk no matter what it's like outside. Here are some tips to keep you safe.

Chapter 11: Finding Room to Roam 167

If you know where to look, you'll find that some of the best areas for walking are just around the corner.

Chapter 12: Finding Time for Fitness 182

Here are some helpful suggestions for fitting fitness into your schedule.

Chapter 13: Spicing Up Your Routine 201

To keep your motivation high, you may want to try these tips for adding a little variety to your walking program.

Chapter 14: Shoes and Accessories 217

You won't get far in your walking program if you don't have the right shoes. Here's what to look for.

Appendix A: Walking Clubs 231

Appendix B: Walking Events 235

Appendix C: Checklists and Reminders 237

Index 249

FROM HERE TO THERE

When you think about it, what is walking? Well, it's a way to get from where you are now to where you want to be—when there's no car, bus, train, or elevator to take you. Walking, however, is more than a means of getting from one location to another. It's a way to get from the shape you're in now to the healthy, fit shape you'd like to have.

Walking can help you attain that trim figure you've been "dieting" to have. It allows you to burn off fat without losing muscle and without depriving your body of the essential nutrients it needs. And it can help tone your muscles and shape up your legs.

Brisk walking is an aerobic exercise; it can train your heart, lungs, and muscles to work more efficiently. And when they're conditioned, they require less oxygen to get their jobs done. That can translate into less strain on your heart and a lower risk of heart disease for you.

Studies have shown that a weight-bearing exercise like walking can strengthen your bones and help ward off osteoporosis, the bone-thinning disease that strikes so many older women. A walking program can help arthritics to maintain flexibility in their affected joints. Regular walking can also play a role in keeping your digestive tract running smoothly.

Frequent walks can boost your energy and help you feel better, calmer, and less stressed all day long. Doctors are even "prescribing" walking as a treatment for depression.

You may have heard similar claims made for other aerobic exercises. But consider this: The only exercise that will do you any good is the exercise you do. And walking is easy—as easy as putting one foot in front of the other. Walking doesn't require great expertise, perfect technique, or a lot of athletic ability. But you've probably already realized that—you took those first steps many years ago.

Walking is inexpensive. It doesn't require loads of heavy-duty equipment. As a matter of fact, a good pair of walking shoes and a watch are probably the only equipment you'll need.

Walking is also convenient. You can walk in the morning, in the evening, or even on your way to work. You can walk alone or with your family, friends, or coworkers. And let's not forget good ol' Spot: Dogs tend to be among the most loyal of walking companions.

One of the best features of walking, however, is its safety record. Walking can be intense enough to boost your aerobic capacity and your overall health, but it's also low-impact. That means it's easy on your joints and safe for people of all ages and fitness levels. If you've been inactive for a long time, walking can safely help you increase your fitness. If you've suffered injuries doing other types of exercise, walking can help you get back on your feet and back into shape. Walking even helps heart attack victims along the road to recovery.

Walk into Shape outlines the health and fitness benefits of walking and provides you with the information you need to walk safely and efficiently. You'll find discussions of how walking can help you lose weight, increase your aerobic fitness, fight off heart disease and other health problems, and help you feel more energetic and less tense.

Walk into Shape also shows you how to prepare your body for a walking program—including tips on making healthy changes in your diet, checking out your health before you hit the road, and preparing for bad-weather and nighttime workouts. You'll even learn how you can use your heart rate as a guide to exercise intensity.

You'll find the Consumer Guide® Walking Programs, complete with easy-to-follow guidelines and handy charts, in Chapter 5. These walking programs have been designed to get you walking and keep you on the road to fitness, no matter what age you are or what kind of shape you are in.

The starter programs allow you to walk at a comfortable pace as you prepare your body for more vigorous exercise. By starting out slowly and progressing gradually, you'll be much less likely to injure yourself and become discouraged. And you'll be much more likely to stay with your walking program—for life.

Once you have mastered the starter programs, you'll advance to the basic walking program. This hearty (and heart-healthy) workout builds aerobic fitness. With this program, you can even adjust the intensity of your walks and the amount of time you spend on each walk to suit your goals and your schedule.

One of the major advantages of a walking regimen is that it can be as flexible as you are. You can make your walking workouts as strenuous as you like. Plain old freestyle walking can be a workout in itself—or a stepping stone to more vigorous walking programs.

If you want more of a challenge, you'll find chapters on racewalking and hiking that will show you how to enhance aerobic benefits, boost the intensity of your workouts, and burn more calories. And although walking is a low-impact activity, accidents can happen. *Walk into Shape* offers advice on prevention and treatment of strains, sprains, and other walking-related injuries.

The key to reaping rewards from any health and fitness program is sticking with it. A good exercise program is one that's enjoyable, flexible, and convenient. In *Walk into Shape*, you'll find chapters designed to keep you from becoming an exercise dropout. You'll find tips on finding pleasant places to walk no matter where you live. You'll learn how to include fitness into a hectic schedule and how to add "spice" to your walking routine.

This book provides you with all you need to know to turn walking into an exercise tool. Of course, you still have to take the first step. Give walking a try and see for yourself how it can improve your fitness and increase your health. It's tough to find a simpler, more enjoyable way to feel healthy—and get from where you are now to where you want to be.

CHAPTER 1

WALKING INTO FITNESS

Has the "no pain, no gain" theory of exercise chased you back to your easy chair? Are you wondering why something that's supposed to be so good for you has to be so uncomfortable and inconvenient? Take heart! Many exercise scientists stress that the key to reaping the health and fitness benefits of physical activity is to choose a regular, moderate exercise program that you can stick with for life. After all, an exercise program won't do you much good if you don't follow it.

So what do you choose? Why not pick the activity that you've been doing all your life? Walking, our natural means of getting from one place to another, provides health and fitness benefits without all that pain. And because of its unbeatable convenience and safety, this low-impact activity has one of the lowest dropout rates of any form of exercise.

Indeed, when scientists first investigated the health and fitness benefits of exercise, it was walking, not running, that they studied. Recently, walking has been "rediscovered" and it's gaining new respect. It is becoming more and more popular as a means to lose and control weight, tone muscles, build strength and endurance, and increase aerobic capacity.

WEIGHT LOSS AND CONTROL

People in search of a lean, healthy look have gone on countless crash diets and lost mountains of fat—only to gain it back again. A series of crash diets that are devoid of exercise strip the body of needed water, muscle, and fat. The fat returns in a flash when the dieting stops, yet only physical activity can rebuild the muscle. The body is left with a lower metabolic rate and a higher risk of future weight gain.

How do you get off the weight-gain roller coaster? After years of studying what works—and what doesn't work—in weight loss and control, the experts seem to have come to some agreement. They now favor lifelong, consistent changes in eating and exercise habits, instead of short-term diets and exercise binges. Although you won't lose weight overnight, the result of the lifelong plan is a sustained increase in the body's percentage of lean body mass (muscle and bone) and a decrease in the body's percentage of fat.

The body usually maintains a delicate balance between the calories taken in as food and those burned up as "fuel." For instance, consuming 2,400 calories of food in a day and burning up 2,400 calories by sleeping, eating, walking, and performing other activities results in neither weight loss nor weight gain. However, if there are any calories left over—if, for example, you take in 2,400 calories and burn only 2,300—they are stored as fat. Storing 3,500 of these extra calories gives you 1 pound of fat. To lose weight, you must use more calories than you consume—by eating fewer calories, by exercising, or, as the experts advise, by combining the two.

When you diet without exercising, your body reacts as if it were being starved, by lowering its metabolic rate. In other words, your body burns fewer calories in order to maintain the weight that its metabolic controls consider healthy and normal. The body may also use protein provided from lean muscle tissue to provide extra calories.

What's more, inactivity can help lead to obesity (defined as weighing 20 percent more than average for your build). People who are obese, in turn, tend to become less active. This compounds their weight problem, completing a vicious cycle in which stress, anxiety, and tension lead to compulsive eating, which results in fat; that extra fat further contributes to inactivity, which begets more weight gain—causing even greater stress, anxiety, and tension.

As mentioned earlier, dieting without exercising also tends to rob the body of lean muscle tissue and water. (Weakness and dark, strong-smelling urine are signs of this muscle wasting.) But the body needs a certain amount of water to avoid dehydration. So when you replenish the water, some of the weight that was lost at the start of the diet is gained back. However, the lean muscle tissue, which contributes to a fit and trim appearance, can only be regained through physical activity. Regular exercise, especially when combined with modest changes in diet, can help you break the vicious cycle of weight gain.

Walking is especially well-suited to play the exercise role. As a sustained, rhythmic workout, walking conserves and may build muscle while it burns calories. And muscle has a higher metabolic rate than fat. So the more muscle and the less fat you have, the more calories you burn while resting.

What about the old myth that exercise defeats the purpose of weight loss because it increases your appetite and makes you eat more? Even the experts don't agree on the exact relationship between appetite and exercise. Several studies suggest, however, that appetite may actually decrease in very sedentary people who begin moderate exercise programs. The important point to remember, however, is that walking burns calories without lowering your resting metabolic rate the way dieting alone does. By burning calories through exercise, you won't need to make such severe changes in your diet. That doesn't mean that you can eat anything you want, however. But you'll be able to enjoy a balanced diet that includes regular meals and enough nutrients to build and maintain a healthy body—and you won't have to starve yourself.

In addition, people who become more active tend to change their food choices spontaneously in a healthier direction, opting for a better-balanced diet with less saturated fat and total calories and more fiber and fresh foods, according to Rose E. Frisch, Ph.D., associate professor of population sciences at the Harvard School of Public Health.

Just how many calories does walking burn? In general, a 150-pound person walking at average speed (from two to three-and-a-half miles per hour) can count on burning about 80 calories a mile. (This amount increases with your weight, your speed, and the shortness of your legs. A 200-pound person burns about one-third more calories than a 150-pound person.) So a brisk walk, covering three-and-a-half miles in an hour, burns about 280 calories. When repeated each day, this excellent habit burns about 3900 calories—more than a pound of fat—every 2 weeks.

This rate of weight loss is a far cry from the "pound-a-day" claims of the crash diets. But when combined with sensible eating habits—a balanced diet with smaller portion sizes and fewer fats and sweets—a walking program can soon translate into a better-looking and healthier body. Weight loss in this moderate range (one or two pounds of fat a week) is easier to maintain. In contrast, higher loss rates tend to involve losses of water and lean muscle, as well as body fat.

If you are out-of-shape or overweight, you should follow a "go-slow" approach when you begin your exercise program. Don't walk at an unrealistic pace; you'll just become exhausted and discouraged, and you may increase your risk of injury. Your goal in walking should be to walk as far as you can for as long as you can. Don't worry about speed. You'll be able to burn more calories by keeping to a moderate pace, exercising for a longer time, and covering more distance.

Walking's weight-loss potential is just as flexible as you are. So as your fitness level increases, you can increase the intensity of your regimen and the number of calories you burn. By walking at a brisk pace of four or five miles per hour and vigorously pumping your arms, or by hiking with a backpack (see Chapter 7), the calories you burn per hour are comparable to those burned in a slow jog.

Indeed, racewalking (see Chapter 6) can actually burn more calories than jogging at the same pace. At high racewalking speeds (like six or seven miles an hour), your body yearns to break into a jog. Forcing yourself to continue walking by keeping at least one foot on the ground at all times takes more energy than jogging at the same speed.

There are also substantial slimming payoffs for tackling hilly terrain. Even at a slow pace, going uphill dramatically raises walking's calorie costs, compared with following the same pace on level ground. Surprisingly, even going downhill burns more calories than covering level ground, because it takes extra energy for the body to resist its natural tendency to travel down the hill too fast. And walking on sand or dirt, rather than rigid asphalt or concrete, can boost the calorie cost by as much as one third.

The advantages of walking don't stop there, either. The warm glow you feel after exercising is a sign that your metabolism is still revved up. This quickened metabolic rate can help you burn a few extra calories after exercise—even while you're resting.

Don't rely solely on the bathroom scale to measure the success of your walking program. Remember, it's fat, not weight, that you really want to lose. Fat is less dense than muscle and it weighs less per unit volume, so it's actually possible to be overfat (with too high a proportion of body fat) without being overweight. The body fat of a healthy male should range from 10 to 18 percent of the total body weight; for a woman, 18 to 25 percent body fat is considered healthy.

Some weight-loss centers, clinics, and fitness clubs now offer body-fat testing, including underwater weighing (based on the principle that fat is more buoyant than lean tissue) and electrical impedance (based on the principle that fat contains much less water than lean tissue, and water conducts electricity). But body-fat testing need not be expensive to be precise. An older, but reliable method is using skin-fold calipers (fat pinchers).

You can also get a pretty good idea of your progress in the war against fat by merely looking in the mirror—and trying on your clothes. This makes more sense than weighing yourself too often (once a week is plenty) or getting too obsessed with what the bathroom scale has to say.

TONING MUSCLES AND BUILDING STRENGTH

You may have noticed that serious walkers have particularly shapely legs—not "toothpick" legs or "thunder thighs." The reason is that walking builds, shapes, and tones muscles all over the legs, hips, and buttocks. Walking also boosts the strength and endurance of those muscles, which means you'll be able to do more with less fatigue.

According to David Winter, Ph.D., professor of kinesiology at the University of Waterloo in

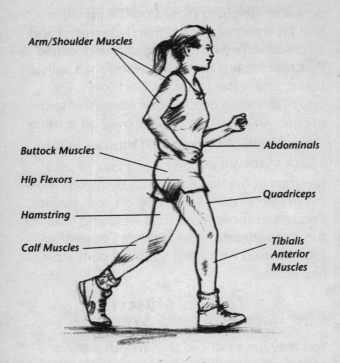

Arm/Shoulder Muscles

Abdominals

Buttock Muscles

Hip Flexors

Quadriceps

Hamstring

Calf Muscles

Tibialis Anterior Muscles

Waterloo, Ontario, Canada, these are the main muscle groups walking affects:

○ Calf muscles—For developing shapely calf muscles, nothing comes close to walking. Walking involves a higher proportion of calf muscle power than does running. The calf muscles provide the upward and forward momentum for the "pushoff" phase of walking, which lifts the heel off the ground.

○ Tibialis anterior muscles—These muscles, which run along the outside of each shin, raise the big toe to flex the foot during the leg's forward motion (or "swing") phase. The muscles then lower the big toe after the heel hits the ground.

○ Hamstring muscles—Walking's pushoff phase works the hamstring muscles in the back of the thighs.

○ Quadriceps muscles—These muscles at the front of the thighs are used as each leg is extended.

○ Hip flexor muscles—The hip flexor muscles lift the leg forward in the "swing" phase of the stride.

○ Buttock muscles—Rocking the hips during brisk walking works your gluteus maximus.

○ Abdominal muscles—Making a point of walking with natural, upright posture can strengthen the abdominal muscles.

○ Arm and shoulder muscles—The arm and shoulder muscles are used when you pump your arms vigorously, up to chest or shoulder level, while walking (the left arm swings forward naturally as the right leg strides ahead, and vice versa).

Methods abound for enhancing the muscle-toning action. You can increase the involvement of the leg-lifting quadriceps by walking uphill—and even downhill. And by lengthening your stride and walking faster, you'll demand more of the hamstrings, hip flexors, and buttocks.

To substantially increase strength and muscle tone in the upper body, however, you'll probably need to do extra exercises, like push-ups and chin-ups. Weight training is also a good way to enhance the strength of both the upper and lower body.

Throughout your walking program, it's very important to stretch your muscles both before and after your walks to maintain your flexibility and ward off injury. In Chapter 8 you'll find a variety of these stretches to choose from and tips on incorporating them into your walking routine.

BUILDING AEROBIC CAPACITY

Like jogging, bicycling, swimming, skating, and cross-country skiing, walking is what is known as an aerobic exercise. That means it is a sustained, repeated, rhythmic workout for large muscle groups. This type of workout requires oxygen and depends on the cardiovascular system to supply this oxygen to the muscles while they work. In contrast, in so-called anaerobic exercises, such as weight lifting or sprinting, the muscles are involved in short bursts of highly intense activity, and they can obtain energy through a chemical process that does not involve oxygen.

Walking at a brisk enough pace offers aerobic benefits by "training" your heart, lungs, and skeletal muscles. Like all muscles, the heart becomes better conditioned the more it is used. By engaging in regular aerobic exercise, you improve your heart's ability to pump oxygen-rich blood to your muscles. You also make your muscles more efficient at using oxygen, so they can do more work without putting as great a strain on your heart. By increasing your aerobic capacity, you make more oxygen available to your body. You'll be able to exercise longer and harder, enabling you to burn more calories during your workouts.

Michael Pollock, Ph.D., director of the University of Florida's Center for Exercise Science, pioneered research on walking's effects on aerobic capacity. He found that walking, jogging, and bicycling all boosted aerobic capacity to the same extent—provided they were done at the same intensity. (The walking group sustained the fewest injuries and had the lowest dropout rate, however.)

It is possible to walk at such a high speed that you equal the aerobic conditioning benefits of jogging. But at usual walking speeds, walking is less intense than jogging, so you've got to walk longer—or uphill—to get the same training effect as you would get by jogging. Another alternative is to use weights—hand-held weights or a backpack—to increase walking's training effects.

For effective aerobic conditioning, you need to walk for a minimum of 30 minutes at least 3 times a week. And during each walk, you need to work hard enough to get your heart rate into your "target range." (See Chapter 4 to learn more about your "target heart rate.")

There's a catch to increasing your aerobic capacity, though. The more fit you are, the faster you must walk to improve your fitness level. This means walking briskly—at least three miles an hour, for most people, and four or more for those already in good shape.

It's long been assumed that people who have already worked themselves from low or average fitness into top condition can't get any fitness training benefits from walking. But Dr. Pollock found that when fit people walked briskly for 40 minutes, four days a week, they could reach a heart-rate range of 70 to 75 percent of their maximum heart rate reserve—close to the results seen with jogging. The difference: If you walk, you need to increase the frequency and duration of exercise to get the same aerobic conditioning results as jogging.

James Rippe, M.D., director of the Center for Health, Fitness and Human Performance at the University of Massachusetts Medical School in Worcester, has made similar findings. Based on his studies of hundreds of walkers, he says even the fittest individuals can raise their heart rates to 70 to 85 percent of maximum, just by walking. But they have to walk fast—as much as six miles per hour—or uphill.

When aerobic conditioning is achieved, it can have important long-term health benefits, including protection against coronary heart disease and stroke. In a Duke University study of 3,000 men, the least fit men were about three-and-a-half times more likely than their healthy counterparts to suffer a fatal heart attack or stroke during an eight-and-a-half year follow-up period.

There is a limit to how much exercise can improve one's aerobic capacity, though, says Ronald LaPorte, Ph.D., associate professor of epidemiology at the University of Pittsburgh. An exercise program can increase a person's aerobic capacity by 30 percent at most. The remaining 70 percent of the aerobic capacity is dictated not by your activity level but by your genes—for such things as lung structure and heart and body size. Because of these variables, it is possible that the aerobic capacity of 2 different people may differ by as much as 200 percent.

WALKING THROUGH PREGNANCY

Doctors often recommend walking as the safest form of aerobic exercise for pregnant women. Women who are habitual walkers are usually urged to continue walking during their pregnancy. Those who have been sedentary are often advised to start a walking program. And those who are accustomed to running may be advised to switch to walking during their pregnancy, to avoid excessive fatigue, breathlessness, and additional stress on the bones and joints. (Hormonal changes in pregnancy tend to loosen ligaments all over the body in preparation for childbirth. As a result, the joints become more susceptible to injury.)

Even though weight reduction is not allowed during pregnancy, walking can help to control excessive weight gain. Walking can also help guard against the development of varicose veins and edema (swelling in the legs and ankles), by increasing circulation. And walking may help alleviate the sway-backed posture (called *lordosis*) that pregnant women can sometimes develop.

With her doctor's OK, after delivery, a new mother can resume her walking routine within a few days.

WALKING AROUND INJURY

One of the biggest problems with strenuous, fitness-boosting exercise is the risk of injury. Although the injury itself may heal in a fairly short time, the damage it does to your motivation and enthusiasm can be longlasting. Fortunately, a walking program can help you increase your fitness with a relatively small risk of injury.

By definition, walking means keeping one foot on the ground at all times. Therefore, compared to jogging, which involves a free-flight phase, walking poses much less danger of falling. And according to Kevin Campbell, Ph.D., a staff scientist at the Cleveland Clinic

Foundation, during walking, each foot hits the ground with a force of only one-and-a-quarter times the weight of the body. In contrast, each running stride lands with a force of up to four times the body weight.

Such high forces on the feet carry stress up the body to the ankle, knee, and hip joints. One study used an artificial hip implant to measure the internal pressure placed on the hip joints during exercise. The stress associated with jogging was one-and-a-half times greater than that found with walking. This explains why so many runners suffer injuries of these joints. In contrast, the lack of these injuries is considered one main reason why walkers are better able to stick with their exercise programs.

In the 1980s, Dr. Pollock discovered that 22 70-year-old people were able to gradually work up to a program of brisk walking with no adverse consequences to either their hearts or their joints. However, when 18 of the subjects then graduated to a program of jogging and jog/walking, 60 percent of them suffered significant injuries. "It was not a cardiovascular limitation, but an orthopedic problem," he stresses.

A regular walking program may even help older adults avoid injury—by keeping them on their feet. For adults over 70 years old, the incidence of injury linked to falls is higher than for any other age group. The neuromuscular changes that occur in aging tend to disturb the sense of balance, which in turn raises the risk of falling and of injury. (Other factors, including medication and osteoporosis, also play a role in the high incidence of injury.) However, participation in a walking program has been shown to improve balance, thereby reducing the risk of falling among older adults.

A well-designed walking program can help anyone achieve higher levels of fitness. Walking can help improve body composition by increasing your body's ratio of muscle to fat. It can help you boost your endurance and increase the strength of the muscles in your lower body. A walking program that includes plenty of stretching exercises can help you maintain flexibility. And, perhaps most importantly, walking can help you increase your aerobic capacity and build a better heart.

CHAPTER 2

WALKING FOR THE HEALTH OF IT

In July 1996, the Surgeon General of the United States issued the latest report on the health of Americans. With the realization that more than half of the U.S. population does not participate regularly in any type of exercise, and that physical inactivity can lead to poor health, the Surgeon General urged Americans to "get in shape," encouraging everyone to get at least one-half hour of moderately vigorous activity each day. The latest recommendations suggest that you should try to walk two miles at a brisk pace of three to four miles per hour nearly every day. If you are able to achieve Level 4 of our Basic Walking Program (see Chapter 5), you are well on your way to meeting the Surgeon General's recommendations.

It is increasingly obvious that one of the best ways to maintain good health is through physical activity. Regular participation in exercise has been shown to prevent such killers as heart disease, cancer, and diabetes. Exercise also helps to control weight. (According to the latest research, one out of three Americans is obese.) And because exercise helps to strengthen muscles and bones, it can even decrease your risk of developing diseases such as osteoporosis and arthritis.

Some of the most interesting and overwhelming evidence supporting the need to be physically active is in the research being conducted at the Cooper Institute for Aerobics Research in Dallas, Texas. Dr. Kenneth Cooper, known as the "father of aerobics," founded the Cooper Clinic in the early 1970s to help people develop healthy lifestyles and investigate the effects of physical activity and fitness on health and longevity.

In July 1996, research from the Cooper Institute showed that participating in moderate to high levels of fitness reduced the risk of dying from any given cause. This held true regardless of other risk factors. In other words, even if an individual suffers from high blood pressure or obesity, the chances of dying are lessened by maintaining a moderate level of fitness. This is remarkably good news, especially for individuals who have hereditary risk factors such as a family history of heart disease.

In 1995, *The Journal of the American Medical Association* published a special report on physical activity and public health. In order to make a recommendation on the amount of exercise necessary to benefit America's health, a panel of experts from the Centers for Disease Control and Prevention and the American College of Sports Medicine (ACSM) reviewed research on physical activity and the impact of exercise on health. Their conclusion was the same as the plea issued by the Surgeon General: "Every U.S. adult should accumulate 30 minutes or more of moderate-intensity physical activity on most, or preferably all, days of the week." The researchers determined that intermittent as well as sustained activity can be beneficial: Don't be overly concerned about days when you don't have time for a 30 minute walk; instead try to fit in shorter walks throughout the day.

This may seem somewhat confusing to those of you who are well acquainted with previous recommendations to exercise for a sustained period of 20 to 60 minutes. The Surgeon General's report is not meant to overshadow or replace these previously recommended exercise guidelines. Exercising for a sustained period of time is still the best way we know to make improvements in your cardiorespiratory fitness. But for many, exercising for long periods of time can be intimidating.

Significant health benefits can be realized by simply ceasing to sit and starting to move. The risk of developing heart disease, high blood pressure, non–insulin-dependent diabetes, and colon and breast cancers can be reduced just by becoming more physically active.

HEART DISEASE

Heart disease is the number one threat to America's health. In fact, 50% of all deaths occurring in the United States each year can be directly attributed to this killer. Scientific evidence suggests that participation in regular physical activity results in a lower risk of developing heart disease. In addition, regular exercise helps individuals recovering from heart attacks and bypass surgery and lowers their risk of suffering a second heart attack.

Heart disease is caused by the build-up of plaque in the coronary arteries. When too much plaque accumulates, blood flow to the heart is decreased. Without enough blood supply, the heart muscle may not get enough oxygen to do its work. Chest pain caused by lack of oxygen to the heart muscle is called *angina*.

People who have angina sometimes use a medication known as nitroglycerin that causes the coronary arteries to dilate, thus increasing the blood flow to the heart and reducing chest pain. When *ischemia* (lack of blood flow to the heart) is caused by a complete blockage of an artery, part of the heart muscle can die. (Complete blockages are often the result of a blood clot that gets caught up in a narrow space in an artery that already has a large build-up of plaque.) This is called a *myocardial infarction,* also known as a heart attack. Sometimes blockages occur in blood vessels that supply blood to the brain. An infarction in the brain is called a *stroke.*

Reducing the risk of heart disease may be your motivation to exercise regularly, particularly if you have risk factors you cannot control. Age and family history of heart disease are both strong risk factors, neither of which are preventable. So if you have had a close family member, such as a parent or sibling, who developed heart disease before the age of sixty, you too are at increased risk. Becoming more physically active and improving your physical fitness improves your chances of living a longer, healthier life.

Physical Inactivity

Physical inactivity is a risk factor for coronary heart disease. When lack of exercise is combined with overeating, excess weight and increased blood cholesterol levels can result—and these conditions unquestionably contribute to the risk of heart disease as well.

Regular exercise has been shown to reduce your resting heart rate, thus decreasing the overall workload on the heart. Some studies show that exercise, combined with a low-fat diet and stress management, can even reduce plaques that have built up in the vessel walls.

Regular aerobic exercise plays a significant role in preventing heart and blood vessel disease. For some years the American Heart Association has recommended 30–60 minutes of aerobic exercise three to four times per week to promote cardiovascular fitness. Such activities could include aerobics, jogging, running, and swimming and sports such as tennis, racquetball, and soccer. Even modest levels of low-intensity physical activity are beneficial if done regularly and long term. Such activities include walking for pleasure, gardening, and housework. Middle-aged or older people should seek medical advice before they start to significantly increase their physical activity.

Cholesterol

Everyone needs a certain amount of cholesterol to build cell membranes and maintain health. But too much of these blood lipids—especially the "bad" low-density lipoprotein (LDL)—can raise your risk for heart disease and stroke. Too little "good" cholesterol (high-density lipoprotein, or HDL), which helps remove fats from the bloodstream, can also pose a problem.

The risk of coronary heart disease rises as blood cholesterol levels increase. If you smoke cigarettes or have high blood pressure, your risk for heart diseases increases even more. A person's cholesterol level can also be affected by age, sex, heredity, and diet.

Nearly everyone can lower their cardiovascular disease risk by eating foods low in saturated fat and adopting an overall healthier lifestyle.

Based on large population studies, blood cholesterol levels below 200 mg/dl (milligrams per deciliter) in middle-aged adults seem to indicate a relatively low risk of coronary heart disease. A level of 240 mg/dl and over approximately doubles the risk. Blood cholesterol levels from 200–239 mg/dl indicate moderate and increasing risk.

HIGH BLOOD PRESSURE

Because you can go for years without knowing you have the condition, high blood pressure has been called the "silent killer." If you have high blood pressure, and you don't control it, your heart has to work progressively harder to pump blood through your arteries. Your heart may enlarge, and you'll be at an increased risk for heart attacks, stroke, kidney failure, and atherosclerosis (buildup of plaque in the arteries).

Men have a greater risk of high blood pressure than women until age 55, when their respective risks become about the same. At age 75 and older, women are more likely to develop high blood pressure than men.

People who have high blood pressure should work with their doctor to control it. Eating a proper diet, losing weight, exercising regularly, restricting salt (sodium) intake, and following a program of medication may all be prescribed to lower blood pressure and keep it within healthy limits.

Your blood pressure is a measurement of the pressure of the blood flow in your arteries. Your systolic blood pressure, the higher number, tells you the pressure in your arteries when your heart is contracting and pumping blood out into the body. Your diastolic blood pressure, the lower number, is the pressure in the arteries when the heart is relaxed. During exercise, your systolic blood pressure increases to improve blood flow, thus increasing available oxygen to the working muscles. Your blood vessels may also become more relaxed, or dilated, to allow for the increased blood flow. This may mean a slight lowering of your diastolic blood pressure. Right after exercise, your blood pressure is probably a little bit lower than before you started. This is a very positive response of the body. Regular exercise has been shown to result in a reduction in blood pressure for those who may be hypertensive.

It is interesting to note that when you stop exercising, your blood pressure will return to its prior level, usually within a week. Therefore, you cannot "bank" your exercise, building up an account, so you can take time off. The benefits of exercise are reduced when you cease to partake of it on a regular basis. A small dosage of exercise done over a long period of time has a much better result than a large amount done irregularly.

Just like you wouldn't want to overdose on medicine, neither would you want to overdose on exercise. If you miss a day or two, don't try to make up for it by overdoing it. Just start your routine again, perhaps even cutting back a little, depending upon how much time you took off.

DIABETES

A regular walking program can help you reduce your chances of developing Type II, or non–insulin-dependent, diabetes. Because a program of regular exercise is extremely helpful in weight management, by reducing the risk of obesity, you also reduce the risk of becoming diabetic. Exercise improves your muscles' ability to respond to insulin and take up more glucose. It can help you reduce your risk of developing diabetes, as well as manage the disease if you already have it. In addition to regular exercise and proper diet, careful monitoring of blood glucose levels is important to diabetes management.

CANCER

Because of the positive impact of exercise on the immune system, exercise can reduce your overall cancer risk. For site-specific cancers, exercise may have a different impact on cancer development. Regular physical activity has been shown to lower the risk of both breast cancer and colon cancer. The mechanism for reduction of breast cancer risk may be due to hormone level changes and reduced body fat that result from exercise. Colon cancer risk may be lowered due to reduced intestinal transit time, thus decreasing the time that possible carcinogens may come in contact with the colon wall.

WALKING AND OSTEOPOROSIS

Osteoporosis is a relatively common disorder characterized by a decrease in the calcium content of the bones, which leaves them thin and susceptible to fracture. The causes of osteoporosis are largely unknown. However, the chances of acquiring the condition seem to increase dramatically with age, especially for women. One prevailing theory maintains that osteoporosis results from a loss of the female hormone estrogen, which affects the calcium content of the bones. Menopause (cessation of menstruation) may lead to osteoporosis because the body's production of estrogen is greatly reduced after that time. Almost one third of all women over the age of 60 experience osteoporosis to some extent.

People who are inactive, either by choice or due to confinement because of illness, seem more susceptible to the disorder. A diet deficient in calcium (which promotes bone development) may also contribute to osteoporosis.

Physicians urge patients with osteoporosis to follow an exercise program that will strengthen the muscles supporting weakened bones. To protect bones in the spinal column, however, lifting heavy objects should be avoided.

QUALITY OF LIFE

Scientists use the term "health related quality of life" to refer to how your health, sense of satisfaction with life, and overall sense of well-being impacts your daily life. People who are physically active obviously enjoy better health. It is also important to note that physically active individuals report feeling better about themselves and have a more positive outlook on life.

CHAPTER 3

LEAVE THE
BLAHS BEHIND

P hysical fitness and increased health are
not the only payoffs of starting and
maintaining a lifelong fitness walking program. Various types of aerobic exercise, including walking, have also been found to
promote mental health—boosting energy,
improving sleep, relieving tension and
stress, and combating anxiety and depression. Mastering a walking program can

give you the true sense of accomplishment that comes from doing something good for your body.

A few years ago, the National Institute of Mental Health (NIMH) convened a panel to examine the effects of exercise on mental health. The panel noted a real, proven link between physical fitness and mental health and well-being. Exercise was deemed generally beneficial for the emotional health of people of all ages and both sexes.

BOOSTING ENERGY

Many people suffer from a type of chronic fatigue that isn't caused by illness or disease. They endure the blahs during the day and then toss and turn at night—only to wake up the next morning feeling groggy and drained. These individuals might be surprised to learn, however, that a great way to increase their daytime energy levels is to expend energy on regular exercise like walking.

In a recent study conducted at the Institute for Aerobics Research in Dallas, aerobic exercises, including fast walking, were found to combat chronic fatigue in 400 men and women who were initially out of shape but who boosted their physical fitness over a two-and-a-half year period. The researchers favor the following scenario to explain this energy rise: Through routine aerobic exercise, the study participants increased their physical fitness, which improved their self-esteem. They felt better about themselves and developed a more optimistic, energetic frame of mind. In addition, the exercisers enhanced the strength and endurance of their muscles and developed the ability to move more efficiently, thus making their daily activities easier to perform—and approach. Other studies have also supported a link between aerobic exercise, enhanced physical stamina, and a more energetic frame of mind.

Several explanations have been proposed for the association between aerobic exercise and increased alertness. Exercise may act by improving circulation and increasing the availability of oxygen to the brain. Increased alertness may also be a side benefit of the raised metabolic rate that occurs during—and after— a bout of exercise. Exercise also causes the body to produce several chemicals, including adrenaline, which promote mental alertness.

IMPROVING SLEEP

Walking can also boost your daytime energy levels by helping you sleep longer and sounder at night. When the President's Council on Physical Fitness asked seven medical experts to rate the sleep-promoting abilities of a whole gamut of physical activities, walking beat out many popular sports, such as handball, squash, basketball, calisthenics, tennis, downhill skiing, softball, golf, and bowling. The only activities that garnered better ratings than walking were jogging, swimming, bicycling, skating, and cross-country skiing.

Some people do find, however, that performing intense exercise just before bedtime revs them up so much that they have difficulty falling asleep. So if you intend to walk at a brisk pace, you may need to schedule your walks for at least an hour before you plan to retire for the evening. On the other hand, an easy-paced, late night stroll may be just the thing to relax your body and clear your mind so you can fall asleep.

RELIEVING STRESS

You're at work. Your boss calls. You have to hand in that big report two weeks early. Your blood pressure surges. Your pulse races. You start seeing red. What are you going to do?

Before you blow up and give the boss a piece of your mind, try going for a stress-busting, lunch-hour walk. Taking time out to pursue an activity like walking can get your mind off distressing concerns and give you a feeling of detachment from daily pressures. By relaxing and giving your mind the room to wander, you may be able to see the situation in a new light. You may even come up with a solution to your dilemma.

Stress can be thought of as the need to adapt to a change. But stress is not always negative. With strong coping strategies, you can handle stress and use it creatively as a call to positive action. Stress-related problems arise when you cannot figure out how to adapt to a stressful situation.

When you feel threatened by a stressful situation, your body automatically prepares you for action. It produces hormones that quicken your pulse, tense your muscles, raise your blood pressure, and sharpen your senses. This "fight or flight" mechanism was a life-saver in earlier times when humans had to cope with physical danger every day. Even today it comes in handy when you're forced into a situation that requires quick action. Unfortunately, most of the stressful situations you're faced with in modern life probably don't require a physical fight or flight. Instead, all this physiological commotion builds up—putting you on edge and keeping you there. Unless you find a way of coping with the situation and relieving the pent-up energy, you leave yourself open to a variety of stress-related psychiatric symptoms, like anxiety, aggression, and depression, not to mention physical ailments such as high blood pressure, tension headaches, and digestive disorders.

At some time, we all need a constructive method of releasing physical energy and emotional stress. Exercise can provide that safety valve. In particular, walking can help relieve stress, thus improving your mood and mental outlook. The NIMH panel on exercise and mental health concluded that exercise can help relieve muscle tension and reduce hormones that serve as messengers of stress. Exercise may also reduce stress-related emotions, including anxiety, anger, aggression, depression, and tension.

A study conducted at the University of Kansas found that people who were physically fit were better able to cope with stressful life changes that had occurred during the previous year. Despite such stressful situations as divorce, death of a loved one, or starting a new job, the study participants who were physically fit complained of fewer health problems and symptoms of depression than did the participants who engaged in little or no exercise.

There are several stress-busting approaches to walking. It can be regarded as a social activity, offering an opportunity to enjoy the company of friends or family. Conversely, it can also be done alone, allowing you the freedom to sort through your thoughts.

If you're stressed-out and plagued by negative, unproductive thoughts, try concentrating on your walking technique and breathing. When you combine walking with taking long, deep breaths, your mind tends to become more aware and alert. You can then choose to invite into your conscious mind only those thoughts that are positive and uplifting. In this way, you can change your whole outlook— easing the way for confidence and peace of mind to replace stress, fear, depression, and anxiety.

To help relieve the myriad of aches and pains associated with stress, such as stiff shoulders and cricks in the neck, special massages and exercises are useful additions to a walking program. Tension-relaxing massage should involve firm but gentle circular strokes, with extra attention to knots and tender spots, especially in the stress-storing shoulders and neck. Stretching exercises such as neck rolls and shoulder shrugs can also help loosen tight muscles.

Walkers can even concentrate on relaxing their muscles as they walk. To do this, simply focus on a particular muscle or muscle group—such as in your shoulders, neck, or jaw. Tense the muscles for a few steps as you walk, then slowly release the tension. As you do this, feel the tightness slipping away.

COMBATING DEPRESSION

Clinical depression is defined as sadness that is greater and more prolonged than is warranted by any objective reason. It is characterized by withdrawal, inactivity, dullness, and feelings of helplessness and loss of control. For many people suffering from clinical depression, regular exercise (three times a week or more appears to work best) has been shown to act as a mood elevator.

Doctors, it seems, are convinced by the evidence in favor of using exercise to treat depression. In a recent survey of 1,750 doctors, 85 percent reported that they prescribed exercise—including walking—for treating depression (and 60 percent prescribed exercise to treat anxiety).

The NIMH panel on the effects of exercise on mental health concluded that long-term exercise reduces depression in people who are moderately depressed. In those who are severely depressed, exercise appears to be a useful addition to professional treatment, including medication, electroshock treatment, and psychotherapy. (Combining exercise with antidepressant medication demands close medical supervision.)

In a University of Wisconsin study, exercise even appeared to be as effective as psychotherapy at relieving moderate depression. People with moderate depression were randomly assigned to either psychotherapy or exercise programs. After a year, over 90 percent of the people who had been assigned to the exercise program were no longer depressed. Half of the patients in the psychotherapy group, however, had come back for more treatment.

Why is walking helpful in the treatment—and perhaps even the prevention—of depression? Following any exercise program, including walking, gives participants a sense of self-reliance, self-mastery, power, and control because they are getting out and doing something for and by themselves, says Robert S. Brown, M.D., Ph.D., clinical associate professor of behavioral medicine and psychiatry at the University of Virginia in Charlottesville. Exercise gives people a real opportunity to set and achieve goals and to see and measure personal improvement. One way to enhance this effect and visualize walking accomplishments is to use a daily log or journal. By writing down the speed of each walk and the distance covered, the walker can keep track of personal improvement.

Walking may also promote feelings of pleasure, tranquility, and well-being and help relieve the pain of depression by encouraging the production of the body's natural opiates, called *endorphins.* These chemical cousins of morphine are responsible for the feeling of euphoria called "runner's high."

Exercise can help distract depressed people from their feelings of sadness. Simply going through the motions of confident striding may be enough to build a walker's confidence. Also, since regular aerobic exercise is an important aid in losing weight and toning muscles, exercisers may feel the general sense of well-being that stems from knowing they look better and feel healthier. And unlike some more strenuous exercises, walking feels good while you're doing it, not just when you stop.

CHAPTER 4

GETTING READY
TO GO

Before you embark on the freestyle walking programs that we've developed,
you need to consider a few preliminaries,
including your overall health, your age,
and your eating habits. You also need to
learn how to measure your heart rate and
listen to your body, so you'll know where
to begin and how hard you need to work
to increase your fitness and health.

CHECKING UP ON YOUR HEALTH

Consult your doctor before you hit the trail or
treadmill, especially if you've been inactive up
to now. Too many Americans have a tendency
to take their health for granted and allow too
much time to elapse between physical examinations. Unfortunately, life-threatening diseases like high blood pressure and coronary
heart disease may not produce symptoms until
a good deal of damage is already done. If you
smoke cigarettes or are overweight, over 45,

or have any significant health problems, your doctor's OK is essential before you begin any exercise program.

The doctor's physical examination should include checking your heart and lungs and taking measurements of your pulse, blood pressure, and blood cholesterol levels. It may also include a resting electrocardiogram, which measures electrical signals from your heart while you are resting.

In some cases, the doctor may decide that you also need an exercise test, which is really nothing more than an electrocardiogram that is taken while you are exercising on a treadmill or stationary bicycle. Doctors often recommend an exercise test to people who have a personal or family history of heart disease because these individuals may have a higher risk of experiencing cardiovascular problems during exercise.

An exercise test is also often recommended for people who are over 45 years old—particularly if they have been inactive; are obese; smoke cigarettes; have high blood pressure, high blood sugar levels, or a high cholesterol level; or have a family history of heart disease. Even if you're under 45, your doctor may give you an exercise test if you have two or more risk factors associated with coronary heart disease or have a history of chest pain.

HEALTH PROBLEMS

If you are overweight or have any significant health problems like arthritis, anemia, lower back pain, foot trouble, diabetes, or a disorder of the heart, lungs, kidney, or liver, you're probably already getting regular medical checkups. Even so, you need to consult your doctor before you begin a walking program to determine if any special precautions need to be considered. For instance, if you have asthma, your doctor may advise you of ways to prevent exercise-induced asthma attacks, especially if you plan to walk outside in cold, dry weather. If you are diabetic or obese, your doctor may want you to add nonweight-bearing activities—like swimming and walking in a pool—to your walking program. If you have insulin-dependent diabetes, your doctor

may advise you of when and where you may
need to take your insulin.

AGING

Your age, in itself, shouldn't keep you from exercising. Many of the physiological changes
that are assumed to be an inevitable part of
aging can actually be linked to inactivity. Regular exercise like walking can actually help you
look and feel younger. However, even the most
active older people cannot avoid all the
changes that occur over time.

For instance, particularly in women, the bones
thin with age and become more susceptible to
injury. This happens, to some extent, no matter how healthy your diet has been or how
much weight-bearing exercise you've done;
the bone-thinning process cannot be pre-
vented entirely. Time also takes its toll on the
joints of the body, with the incidence of arthritis climbing in the later years.

For these reasons, people over the age of 45
should consult a doctor and have a checkup
before starting any new exercise program.

EATING RIGHT

To make the most of your health and fitness,
you need to do more than exercise regularly.

You also need to eat a sensible, well-balanced diet that includes a variety of healthy foods. After all, you can't expect your body to work well if you don't supply it with the nutrients it needs. And you can't expect to greatly improve your health or your figure with poor eating habits. So before you take to the road, take a look at your diet.

The Dietary Guidelines for Americans, published by the USDA, recommend following a diet that is low in fat and cholesterol and high in complex carbohydrates, such as bread, potatoes, cereals, and pasta. According to the 1995 Guidelines, about 60 percent of the calories you consume should come from carbohydrates, 15 percent from protein, and less than 30 percent from fat. You need to pay attention to the type of fat you consume, too. No more than 10 percent of your total calories should come from saturated fats, like those in meat, dairy products, and coconut and palm oil; no more than 10 percent should come from polyunsaturated fats, like those in soft margarine, mayonnaise, corn oil, sunflower oil, and safflower oil; and the rest should come from monounsaturated fats, like those in chicken, fish, peanut butter, vegetable shortening, and olive oil. You should also limit your cholesterol intake to less than 300 milligrams (mg) per day. Cholesterol is found in many animal products and in some foods high in saturated fat.

In contrast, most Americans now eat less carbohydrates and more cholesterol and fat—particularly saturated fat, which has been fingered as a major culprit in coronary heart disease. The average American consumes about 37 percent of total calories in fat, including as much as 15–20 percent from saturated fat. Although the average American eats a healthier diet today than ten years ago, there is still room for improvement.

You don't have to starve yourself or give up all of your favorite foods in order to improve your eating habits. Instead, you can make gradual, moderate changes in your diet—such as switching from whole milk to low-fat milk or eating fish two times a week—to help lower your risk of coronary heart disease and control your weight.

One easy way to keep track of what you're eating and improve your food choices is to refer to the Food Guide Pyramid. The accompanying chart illustrates the Food Guide Pyramid and provides suggestions for choosing the healthiest foods from each group.

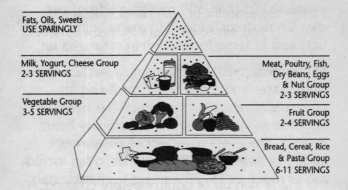

Fats, Oils, Sweets
USE SPARINGLY

Milk, Yogurt, Cheese Group
2-3 SERVINGS

Meat, Poultry, Fish,
Dry Beans, Eggs
& Nut Group
2-3 SERVINGS

Vegetable Group
3-5 SERVINGS

Fruit Group
2-4 SERVINGS

Bread, Cereal, Rice
& Pasta Group
6-11 SERVINGS

The Food Pyramid is an excellent dietary guide, particularly for active people. The active person requires a diet fairly high in complex carbohydrates (from grains, cereals, fruits, and vegetables) to supply the energy necessary for exercising.

In addition to the Food Guide Pyramid, the following recommendations from the American Heart Association can help you make gradual changes in your cooking and eating habits:

❍ Eat a variety of foods from the various food groups to help you get all the nutrients you need and to keep mealtime from becoming a bore.

❍ Choose lean cuts of meat and trim any visible fat.

- Limit the amount of lean meat, fish, and poultry you eat to no more than six ounces a day.

- Substitute vegetable proteins such as dried beans, peas, or legumes for meat proteins as often as you can.

- Choose fish, poultry, and veal more often than beef, lamb, or pork.

- Trim the skin off of poultry before cooking.

- Substitute skim milk and low-fat cheeses for whole milk products.

- Try substituting two egg whites for one whole egg in recipes.

- Avoid frying foods. Instead, use cooking methods that help remove fat, such as baking, boiling, broiling, roasting, or stewing.

You should probably wait at least two hours after you eat to begin an intense bout of exercise. (A light stroll would be alright as long as you feel comfortable and not overly full from your meal.) Otherwise, if you are too full or have consumed too much fat, your digestive tract will be competing with your working muscles for oxygen-carrying blood. Usually, the muscles win out, interfering with digestion, making you feel bloated and sometimes causing cramps.

The best meal to eat before a long or intense walking workout is one high in complex carbohydrates—rather than fat or protein, which take longer to digest. Sugar (a simple carbohydrate) is no substitute for these complex carbohydrates; nor is it a good idea to eat foods high in sugar shortly before exercising. Despite popular lore, loading up on sugar will not help fuel your activity, because it takes about 20 to 30 minutes for the energy from the sugar to be made available to your muscles. A pre-exercise sugar binge can also cause a surge of insulin, which paradoxically results in low blood sugar during the activity—and that can seriously hinder your performance.

Exercise does not significantly raise a person's requirements for protein or for most vitamins and minerals. (Exercise does slightly increase the need for the B vitamins, which can be obtained by eating whole-grain or enriched cereals.) So there is no reason for the active person to load up on extra protein servings or to gulp down vitamin or mineral supplements.

It is particularly important for the active person to drink plenty of water, however. You should drink water before, during, and after exercise—particularly in warm weather—even if you don't feel thirsty. As a thirst quencher, water is tough to beat.

FOLLOWING YOUR HEART

The walking programs in the next chapter will take you step-by-step down the road to increased health and fitness. But since your body is like no one else's, you'll need your own personal guide to tell you where to begin and how much physical effort to contribute. Your best bet? Follow your heart and listen to your body. Your heart rate can tell you when you're working hard enough to increase your aerobic fitness. Your body lets you know how hard you are working: If it feels like too much to you, you're probably pushing too hard.

Exercise physiologists have figured out a heart rate range that is safe for most people during exercise. They call this your *target heart rate range.* This range tells you your optimum level of exertion during exercise. That doesn't mean you can't get any health or fitness benefits by exercising below or above that range. It's just that keeping your heart rate in the target range during regular aerobic exercise has been shown to be safe and effective for increasing your aerobic fitness. Exercising above this range can be very uncomfortable and may increase your risk of injury. In fact, if you've been inactive, it's best to start gradually, with a heart rate that may even be below your target heart rate range.

To find your target heart rate range, you first need to know your maximum heart rate. An exercise test can give you this information. But if you haven't taken an exercise test, you can get an estimate of your maximum heart rate by subtracting your age from 220. For example, if you are 25 years old, your maximum heart rate is 220 minus 25, or about 195 beats per minute. If you're 48 years old, your maximum heart rate is 220 minus 48, or about 172 beats per minute. Your actual maximum heart rate can vary by as many as 25 beats per minute. If you are older or have heart problems, therefore, it may be a good idea to have an exercise test performed at your doctor's office to find out your precise maximum heart rate.

YOUR TARGET HEART RATE RANGE

By exercising within your target range for at least 20–30 minutes, three or more days a week, you can safely and effectively increase your aerobic fitness. We recommend that you work up to the target range gradually by following the walking programs outlined in the next chapter.

To check your heart rate, you need a watch that measures seconds, not just minutes. You can take your pulse either at the radial artery in your wrist (on the inner side of your wrist, below the heel of your hand) or the carotid artery in your neck (just to the side of the throat). Use the index and middle fingers of one hand to feel the pulse. If you use the artery in your neck, however, place your fingers gently; putting too much pressure on this artery can actually slow down your pulse and give you a false reading. When you've found your pulse, count the number of beats for ten seconds. Then multiply that number by six to find your heart rate in beats per minute. If you have trouble taking your pulse, you may want to purchase an inexpensive stethoscope that allows you to hear your heartbeat or use an automated pulse taker.

To find your optimum level of exertion during exercise, use your maximum heart rate reserve. Exercising at 40 percent to 85 percent of your maximum heart rate reserve will give you a healthy aerobic workout. We've outlined a simple formula that you can use to calculate it:

Step One: Measure your resting heart rate by counting your pulse for ten seconds and multiplying that number by six. (Be sure to do this when you're resting.)

Step Two: Subtract your resting heart rate from your maximum heart rate. (You can find your maximum heart rate by subtracting your age from 220 or by performing an exercise test.)

Step Three: Multiply the result of step two by .4 (40 percent) and add that to your resting heart rate to find the lower limit of your maximum heart rate reserve target zone.

Step Four: Multiply the result of step two by .85 (85 percent) and add that to your resting heart rate to find the upper limit of your maximum heart rate reserve target zone.

You can use this method as a guide throughout the walking programs in the next chapter. By exercising at 40 percent to 85 percent of your maximum heart rate reserve for at least 20–30 minutes a day, 3 times a week or more, you can develop and maintain your aerobic fitness. Since freestyle walking is a moderately intense exercise, however, you may not be able to reach the upper limit of these ranges, according to Dr. Pollock, who helped draft the *American College of Sports Medicine's Guidelines for Fitness in Healthy Adults.* So you may have to walk longer (for at least 30 minutes) and more often (or progress to racewalking or walking with weights) to achieve the same benefit as you would by exercising at a higher heart rate.

As you'll see, the walking programs in this book are designed to get you to your optimum level of exercise gradually. At first, you'll walk at a comfortable pace, one that may not get your heart rate in the target zone. Then you will gradually work your heart rate into the target zone. By progressing slowly, you'll decrease your risk of injury. You'll also be more likely to stick with the exercise program. As your fitness increases, you will notice two telltale signs. It will take more exercise—or more intense exercise—to raise your heart rate into the target zone. And your resting heart rate will decline.

A word of caution: Don't be a slave to your pulse, measuring it so often that it becomes a compulsion. Don't let taking your pulse destroy your sense of fun and spontaneity in exercise. When you first begin your walking program, you may want to take your pulse as often as every 10 or 15 minutes so that you can get a feel for how hard your body is working. As you progress through the program, you can take your pulse every 20 to 30 minutes to be sure you're working in your target range. In time, you may only need to check your pulse at the beginning and end of your walk; you may be able to tell whether you're working in your target range just by the way you feel.

As a matter of fact, one of the tools used by exercise scientists to measure and prescribe exercise is something called the rating of perceived exertion (RPE) scale. The exerciser rates how hard he or she feels the exercise is, using a 15-point scale that goes from 6 (resting) to 20 (very, very hard). This rating scale has been found to correlate well with physiological indicators of fatigue or strain, including heart rate and oxygen uptake. In other words, you can use your perception of how hard you're working as a guide. If you really feel like you're walking at a

Borg's RPE Scale	
6	No Exertion at All
7	Extremely Light
8	
9	Very Light
10	
11	Light
12	
13	Somewhat Hard
14	
15	Hard (Heavy)
16	
17	Very Hard
18	
19	Extremely Hard
20	Maximal Exertion

moderately intense pace, you probably are; a measurement of your heart rate would probably confirm that you're working in the moderately intense range of 40 percent to 85 percent of your maximum heart rate reserve. By checking your pulse more frequently during the early stages of your walking program, you'll get a feel for how your body reacts to different levels of exertion; later, you'll be able to judge your exertion without having to stop and check your pulse every ten minutes.

LISTEN TO YOUR BODY

There are three more principles that can guide you through your walking program. They should help you fight any tendency you may have to push yourself too hard. Remember, walking is an ideal activity to keep up for the rest of your life. You've got plenty of time to build up to a more demanding stride.

First is the "talk test," which is especially important during your first six weeks of walking. The talk test means that you should be able to hold a conversation with someone as you walk. If you are too winded to talk, you can probably conclude that you're walking too fast for your present fitness level. Even if you walk alone, you can use your imagination. Do you feel like you could keep up a conversation? If not, you may want to slow down.

Second, your walk should be painless. If you experience pain or a feeling of heaviness in your chest, jaw, neck, feet, legs, or back, you should see your doctor and describe what happened. Try to recall the circumstances: "I was walking up a hill," "It happened during the first few minutes," or "The weather was very cold."

Third, if you seem excessively tired for an hour or more after your walk, the walk was too strenuous. Your walk should be exhilarating, not fatiguing. If you experience a dizzy or light-headed feeling, it's time to back off. If you feel nauseous or are tired for at least a day after walking, take it easy. If you can't sleep at night or if your nerves seem shot, it means that you've been pushing too hard. The same is true if you seem to have lost your "zing" or can't catch your breath after a few minutes of walking. These are your body's warning signs. If you have any questions about excessive fatigue, pain, or discomfort, see your doctor.

When walking, remember to listen to your body. It may take some practice, but you'll learn that your body really can tell you when to speed up or slow down.

CHAPTER 5

FREESTYLE FITNESS WALKING

Perhaps the best thing about walking is that you are already an expert at it. You probably acquired your walking skills quite some time ago. In this chapter, however, we'll show you how to turn your walking skills into an exercise tool that can tune up your body and improve your health.

The programs we've developed allow you to start out your walking program slowly and progress without strain, no matter what shape you're in. The programs are demanding enough to help you improve your fitness, but flexible enough for you to adapt them to your individual abilities and your daily routines.

You can use them to prepare for a lifetime of freestyle walking or as a start-up step to get your body in gear for racewalking or hiking. (See Chapters 6 and 7 for more on these unique types of walking.)

WALKING STYLE

The "secret" to walking comfortably is to walk naturally—pretty much as you've been walking up to now. Don't be too concerned with proper walking style for these freestyle walking programs. Remember, your body is unique. It has its own particular form and style, so you can't force it to behave like someone else's body. Just walk naturally and enjoy yourself.

It is a good idea, however, to keep your spine straight and to hold your head high as you walk. You can walk into trouble—in the form of cars, trees, and other people—if you stare at the ground. Try not to be so conscious of your posture that you feel unnatural, though. Forget the ramrod-straight posture encouraged in the military, where the chest is thrown out and the back hyperextended. This posture doesn't allow your back and hips to move to accommodate the natural shift of your weight from one leg to the other. Instead, keep your wrists, hips, knees, and ankles relaxed. Allow your arms to hang loosely at your sides. They will swing naturally in opposite action to your legs—the left arm sweeping forward as the right leg strides ahead, and vice versa. (Race-walkers use a unique form that helps them to walk at high speeds. Refer to Chapter 6 if you would like to learn more about racewalking.)

As you walk, each foot should strike the ground at the heel. You then transfer your weight forward from your heel, along the outer portion of your foot, to your toes. To complete the foot-strike pattern, you push off with your toes. As you shift your weight from heel to toe, you should get a rolling motion. Avoid landing flat-footed or on the balls of your feet. If you do, you may be headed for leg and foot problems later on.

As you begin your walking program, don't worry about the length of your stride. Just do whatever is comfortable. As you increase your speed, your stride length will increase as well.

Breathe naturally as you walk, using both your nose and your mouth. Remember that the faster you go, the more air you'll need. So help yourself to all the air you want.

Don't follow these guidelines slavishly. It's likely that the way you walk now is best for you. However, if you do experience any pain or discomfort while you walk, you may need to make an adjustment in your walking technique or switch to a different pair of walking shoes. (You'll find more about walking pain and its various causes in Chapter 9.) If you have further questions, see your doctor. Remember, you're not competing in the Olympics. You're walking for fun and fitness.

WARMING UP AND COOLING DOWN

As with any exercise program, each workout in your walking program should start with a warm-up period and end with a cool-down period. You can achieve this by starting each walking workout with five minutes or more of slow walking, followed by a series of stretches. Then, after walking at your regular pace, end your workout with a five-minute slow walk, followed by another series of stretches. (See Chapter 8 for more on warm-up and cool-down exercises and stretches.) These steps are essential parts of your walking program. They will help you maintain your flexibility and prevent pain or injury. Warming up, cooling down, and stretching all become even more important if you graduate to more demanding workouts that involve striding, racewalking, or walking up and down hills. The greater intensity of these workouts increases your risk of injuring tight muscles.

HOW TO GET STARTED

To get yourself started and keep yourself walking, you need a plan that puts you on a regular walking schedule. Our step-by-step program really works. It will help you increase your health and fitness while you experience the true pleasures of walking. You'll find this program demanding enough to get the job done, yet flexible enough to be adapted to your particular needs, age, present level of fitness, and lifestyle.

Getting started doesn't require any elaborate planning or expensive equipment—just a comfortable pair of well-constructed walking shoes to support and cushion your feet and prevent them from turning inward too much when they hit the ground. (See Chapter 14 about what to look for when purchasing walking shoes.) Don't forget to warm up and stretch before you actually hit the trail.

BASIC STARTER PROGRAM

The Consumer Guide® Basic Starter Program is a good way to prepare your body for more demanding exercise. If you find the Basic Starter

Program too difficult or if you have heart, lung, or joint problems, you should begin with the Special Starter Program on page 75.

The following table summarizes the Basic Starter Program.

Level 1: Walk 20 minutes a day 3 to 5 times a week.

Level 2: Walk 25 minutes a day 3 to 5 times a week.

Level 3: Walk 30 minutes a day 3 to 5 times a week.

Level 4: Walk 35 minutes a day 3 to 5 times a week.

Level 5: Walk 40 minutes a day 3 to 5 times a week.

Level 6: Walk 45 minutes a day 3 to 5 times a week.

In this starter program, you should walk fast enough to get your heart rate into the lower end of your target zone—about 60 percent of your maximum heart rate or about 50 percent of your maximum heart rate reserve (see Chapter 4 to learn how to find your target heart rate). If you find that you can't walk comfortably at that pace for the specified amount of time, then slow down. Stay at each level until you can keep your heart rate in the lower end of your target zone for the specified amount of time, then proceed to the next level. The key is always to listen to your body. You may need to spend two weeks at each level, or maybe a week at one level and two weeks at another. If, however, you find that walking at even a very slow pace for 20 minutes is too difficult for you, then switch to the Special Starter Program.

Try not to get impatient and skip ahead, even if you find the Basic Starter Program too easy. (You should spend at least one week at each level.) Stick with it—slow and steady. You'll be glad you did, because this approach will raise the odds that you'll continue with your walking program. Remember, anybody can start an exercise program, but not everyone can stay with it. Your primary goal in this starter program is to get motivated to exercise on a regular basis. Once you've completed it, you can proceed to the Basic Walking Program.

SPECIAL STARTER PROGRAM

The Consumer Guide® Special Starter Program is designed for people who find the Basic Starter Program too difficult or who have health problems.

Level 1: Walk 10 minutes a day 3 to 5 times a week.

Level 2: Walk 12 minutes a day 3 to 5 times a week.

Level 3: Walk 14 minutes a day 3 to 5 times a week.

Level 4: Walk 16 minutes a day 3 to 5 times a week.

Level 5: Walk 18 minutes a day 3 to 5 times a week.

Level 6: Walk 20 minutes a day 3 to 5 times a week.

In the Special Starter Program, you should begin by walking at a comfortable pace, even if it doesn't elicit your target heart rate. Begin at a level that feels comfortable and stay there for at least one week, then proceed to the next level.

If, however, the Level 1 duration of ten minutes, three to five times a week is too difficult—for instance, if you're out of breath as you walk—then start by walking five minutes a day or less. Some emphysema patients walk for only a minute or two at the start. You be the judge.

Once you can walk without discomfort for 20 minutes a day, 3 to 5 times a week, move on to the Basic Starter Program. From there, you will eventually graduate to the Basic Walking Program.

BASIC WALKING PROGRAM

Once you've completed the Basic Starter Program, you are ready for bigger and better things, including walking faster and getting your heart rate well into your target range. Now it's time for you to begin the Basic Walking Program, summarized in the following table.

Level 1: Walk 20 minutes a day 3 to 5 times a week.

Level 2: Walk 25 minutes a day 3 to 5 times a week.

Level 3: Walk 30 minutes a day 3 to 5 times a week.

Level 4: Walk 35 minutes a day 3 to 5 times a week.

Level 5: Walk 40 minutes a day 3 to 5 times a week.

Level 6: Walk 45 minutes a day 3 to 5 times a week.

Level 7: Walk 50 minutes a day 3 to 5 times a week.

Level 8: Walk 55 minutes a day 3 to 5 times a week.

Level 9: Walk 60 minutes a day 3 to 5 times a week.

In the Basic Walking Program, your aim is to get your heart pumping at 50 percent to 85 percent of your maximum heart rate reserve. Of course, as your fitness increases, you can't expect to just shuffle along and reach this heart rate range. You'll have to walk at a good clip.

As in the Basic Starter Program, you need to stay at each level until you can walk at that pace for the specified amount of time.

Once you've reached Level 9 (or Level 6 if you're short on time) of this program, you can maintain your fitness level by walking in your target range for at least 30 to 45 minutes a day, at least 3 times a week.

While these programs provide guidelines for how much exercise you need to do to improve your health and fitness, your own fitness goals can help you choose the exact duration, frequency, and speed of your walks. For instance, if your main goal is to lose weight, you may choose to walk for 45 minutes to an hour, 5 times a week, at 65 percent to 70 percent of your maximum heart rate reserve. By keeping to a more moderate pace (yet still in your target zone), you'll be able to walk for a longer period of time.

Remember, the longer you walk, the more calories you'll burn. There's a simple rule of thumb to follow: If you decrease the speed of your walks, increase their duration and frequency. You can adjust how often, how long, and how fast you walk to suit your goals, as long as you keep your heart rate somewhere within your target zone and exercise for a minimum of 30 minutes a day, at least 3 times a week.

If you find yourself missing the slower pace of the starter program and the chance it gave you to savor your surroundings, you may want to alternate brisk walks with more leisurely ones. You might try confining brisk walking to 30 minutes or so in the middle of your workout, sandwiched between long, slow warm-up and cool-down periods. You may also want to walk up and down hilly terrain, so that you can increase the intensity of your workout without having to walk at high speeds.

Of course, you don't have to restrict your walking to your "official" workout times. Instead, you can try taking full advantage of the opportunities that each day offers for extra walking. For instance, try walking up and down stairs at every chance you get, instead of taking an elevator or escalator. Walk to the post office instead of driving there. (For ideas on how to find more time for walking, see Chapter 12.) Remember, any walking you can do in addition to your scheduled workouts is an added bonus in terms of health and fitness.

For the sake of convenience, it is important to build your walks into your daily schedule of activities (see Chapter 12). To keep your motivation high and your walks interesting, you may want to vary the routes you choose to roam (see Chapter 11) or add new dimensions to your walking routine (see Chapter 13).

Once you have mastered the Basic Starter Program and the Basic Walking Program, you may decide you want to be further challenged. Or you may be so fit that you have trouble walking fast enough to push your heart rate well into your target zone. If so, you can increase the intensity of your workouts by learning to racewalk (see Chapter 6), which will enable you to reach higher walking speeds. You may also want to try increasing the time and distance you walk by taking up hiking (see Chapter 7).

SPECIAL HEALTH CONSIDERATIONS

If you're recovering from a heart attack, walking can help you down the road to recovery. Talk to your doctor about beginning an exercise regimen using the Special Starter Program. Your doctor will help you establish your target heart rate and advise you on any precautions you need to consider before beginning a walking program.

CHAPTER 6

RACEWALKING

Once you've worked your way through the freestyle walking programs in Chapter 5, you may be interested in accelerating your program to get even more of an aerobic workout. Perhaps you want to pick up speed. Or maybe you're craving competition. If so, learning to racewalk may be a natural next step for you. By using the technique of racewalking, you'll be able to move faster and raise your heart rate well into the target range, even if you are already quite fit.

Racewalking can maximize your walking workout. Here's why: At racewalking speeds of five miles per hour or more, it is actually more efficient for your body to jog than to walk. You can experience this for yourself. Try walking as fast as you can, and you'll feel your body aching to jog. In order to continue walking and not break into a jog, you have to keep one foot on the ground at all times. You can't use that gliding motion—when both feet are off the ground—that allows joggers to cover more distance with each step. So in order to cover the same distance, you have to take more steps than you would if you were jogging.

WHY RACEWALK?

At high speeds, racewalking actually involves a higher rate of muscle activity and burns more calories per mile than does jogging at the same pace. According to James Rippe, M.D., of the University of Massachusetts, racewalking burns 120 to 130 calories per mile—that's more than running (which burns between 100 and 110) and certainly more than freestyle walking.

Racewalking also gives your upper body a healthy workout. In order to walk at high speeds, you have to pump your arms vigorously. This movement helps tone and strengthen the muscles in your arms, neck, and chest as it burns calories.

All this extra activity shows up in increased health and fitness benefits. Indeed, elite competitive racewalkers have physiological profiles that are comparable to those of distance runners. They have low body fat and a high ratio of "good" to "bad" cholesterol, according to a recent study conducted at Wayne State University in Detroit.

Another advantage of racewalking is that it can be practiced as a competitive sport and it's an excellent way to add challenge to your walking program. It can be practiced and enjoyed in or out of competition. (See Appendix A for more information on racewalking clubs and events.)

Racewalking does put greater stress on the ankle, knee, and hip joints than does freestyle walking, however. (Whenever you increase the intensity of an exercise, you increase the risk of injury.) But the strain is less than that caused by jogging, because you always have one foot on the ground when you racewalk.

You can lower your risk of injury by beginning your program slowly and increasing your speed gradually; by doing plenty of stretches and allowing your body to warm up before you begin each walk; and by following proper racewalking form. (See Chapter 8 for more information on both stretching and strengthening exercises.)

Proper Racewalking Form

You may have seen racewalkers on television or watched them "wiggle" past you in the local park. You may have wondered about their unusual technique—vigorously pumping arms and exaggerated hip action. Some people find it comical, but racewalkers know that it's this unique form that allows them to reach high walking speeds.

Racewalkers generally walk at speeds ranging from about five miles per hour to about nine miles per hour (walking at speeds of five miles per hour or more without using the racewalking technique is very difficult, if not impossible, for most people). Record-setting elite racewalkers, however, have achieved astounding speeds nearing ten-and-one-half miles per hour.

As you begin to racewalk, however, it is important to concentrate more on the proper form, which is no cinch to master, than on speed. Speed will come later, as you master the racewalking technique.

There are three main features of racewalking form; they're in the official rules that govern the sport. Those rules, according to the International Amateur Athletic Federation, state that:

1. One foot must be in contact with the ground at all times.

2. There must be a two-leg support period during each cycle of pushing off, swinging, and weight acceptance.

3. The weight-supporting leg must be straight for at least one moment when it's in the vertically upright position.

In other words, in racewalking, you must have one foot touching the ground at all times. The heel of your front foot must touch the ground before the toes of your back foot leave the ground. And, during your stride, the leg that is supporting your weight must be straight for at least a moment as your torso passes directly over it.

As you incorporate all of these movements into your form, you probably will be walking at a fairly slow pace. That's fine for this stage. Just walk at a pace that's comfortable and focus on your form. Once you feel comfortable with these movements, you can begin to increase your speed and raise your heart rate into your target zone. Be sure, however, to increase your speed gradually. Don't push too hard or walk to the point of exhaustion.

RACEWALKING FORM

Are you interested in learning to racewalk and maximizing your walking workout? Follow these steps and learn the correct racewalking form:

Step 1: As the body passes over the torso, the supporting leg is straight in the upright position. The opposite leg is moving forward, with the foot close to the ground. Note that the arm is bent at a 90 degree angle.

Step 1

Step 2: The supporting leg is beginning to push the body ahead, causing the body to lean forward slightly. The opposite hip and leg are swinging forward, with the foot close to the ground. The arm above the supporting leg is beginning its upward thrust.

Step 2

Step 3: The supporting leg is exerting a strong push as the body leans forward. The opposite hip and leg are reaching forward. The arm above the supporting leg is pumping across the chest as the opposite arm pumps back.

Step 4: In this final step, the supporting leg continues to push the body forward as the heel of the opposite foot touches the ground. Note that the foot of the supporting leg is still in contact with the ground as the back of the opposite heel makes contact. Notice that the arms are at the high point of their pumping motion.

Step 3

How do you adjust your form to incorporate these features? Stand straight, with your toes aimed dead ahead. Begin walking by stepping forward with your left hip, your left knee, and your left heel. Be sure you land first on the back edge of your heel. Your left foot should be at a 90 degree angle to your left leg (your leg and foot should form the shape of a capital "L"), and your heel should be at about a 40 degree

Step 4

angle to the ground. When the back edge of your heel strikes, tilt your foot ever-so-slightly toward the outer edge of your shoe; you'll be rolling on the outer edge of your foot as you shift your weight from the back to the front of your foot. This will keep your knee from rotating inward, which can cause "runner's knee."

As your left leg lands and begins to pull you forward, give yourself a strong pushoff with your right foot. As your right foot leaves the ground and begins to swing forward, your torso will pass directly over your left leg. At that moment, your left leg must be straight. Once your torso has passed directly over your left leg, your left leg will push you forward until the back of your right heel strikes the ground.

You should keep a few things in mind as you practice this technique. First, be sure to keep your toes pointing straight ahead as you walk. If you don't, you'll be moving from side to side as well as forward, wasting energy and losing speed.

Second, pay attention to foot placement. In freestyle walking, your feet land about shoulder-width apart (in the side-to-side direction). In racewalking, your feet should line up one behind the other. To practice this, try walking an imaginary straight line (or draw a straight line on the pavement with chalk). As you extend each leg forward, try to plant it on the line, or as close to the line as possible. This will keep you from waddling and give you a smooth, efficient stride.

Third, when your supporting leg is straight, the hip above it should rise and relax. This will let the bones of the leg support the weight and give the muscles a break. This hip movement can be somewhat hard to achieve at first, particularly for men who are "trained" to believe that mobile hips are feminine-looking. But the hip movement is crucial to the racewalker, because it makes the stride as smooth as possible. Also, as you swing the nonsupporting leg forward, be sure to swing the hip above it forward, too.

Finally, as you walk, you should feel yourself leaning forward from the ankles. Don't bend forward at the waist, however. This will strain your back and neck and could hamper your breathing.

In addition to using your legs and hips correctly, you need to get your arms in on the act. As in freestyle walking, your arms will naturally swing to counterbalance your legs. But if you consciously and vigorously pump your arms, you can actually help your legs move faster. To get the most benefit, keep your arms bent at right angles. Pump your arms diagonally across the center of your body, keeping your elbows close to your sides. Don't pump your arms too high, however—chest-high is enough.

STRETCHING

Before you begin each workout, even when you're just practicing your form, you need to warm up your body and stretch your muscles. The same goes for after each workout. If you neglect these important steps, you may be in for some serious muscle pain and perhaps even injury.

Before you begin your racewalking workout, walk slowly and casually (not in racewalking form) for a few minutes to warm up your muscles. Then stop and stretch. In Chapter 8, you'll find various stretches to choose from. Stretches that involve the upper and lower body are important, because so many of the body's muscles are involved in racewalking. Stretch your muscles gently, without bouncing or pulling to the point of pain. Once you've completed your walk, stretch again to help maintain your flexibility.

Even with proper stretching, you may feel some soreness early in the program. That's to be expected, since you may not have used some of those muscles in a while. (Be sure to pamper your muscles with massages and warm baths.) Don't walk to the point of pain, however. If pain or discomfort persists, see your doctor.

Since racewalking is such a specialized activity, and so distinct from freestyle walking and jogging, shoes have been designed specifically for the sport (see Chapter 14).

ENTERING COMPETITION

A large number of local, national, and international racewalking competitions are held each year, covering distances from 1 mile to 31 miles (50 kilometers). These events allow you the opportunity to test out your speed and your form.

You could, of course, enter running races or marathons and racewalk your way through. This way, you wouldn't be judged on technique, but you would still be competing. As you increase your speed and skill, you may even find yourself passing some of the runners, especially in longer events.

Whichever type of competition you choose, it's best to begin with shorter, slower races. Stay away from very short sprinting races, however; you might be tempted to push yourself too hard too soon. You may want to try a more moderately paced four-mile event first. In order to progress to longer or faster races, you'll need to prepare yourself—increasing your speed and distance gradually in your training sessions.

Before you begin entering races, you may want to attend a racewalking event as a spectator. By watching the competitors, you may be able to pick up tips for perfecting your form. You may also get the opportunity to ask the racers (or even the judges) for advice on proper racewalking form.

HIKING

Stepping up your pace is one way to build the intensity of your workouts. But as discussed in Chapter 5, if walking quickly is too uncomfortable, you can opt for longer walks at a more moderate pace. In terms of energy costs, a day-long hike up hills and down winding paths is similar to running a marathon. But when it comes to taking in the sights, smells, and sounds as you go, hiking is tough to beat.

WHERE TO GO

Where you choose to hike will depend, in part, on your interests. If you enjoy watching birds, for example, you may want to pack your binoculars and head for a swampy area like the

Everglades National Park, which is known for its ornithological richness. If you're interested in plant life, you may want to plan a spring or summer hike in the Great Smoky Mountains National Park, where you'll find a brilliant display of rhododendrons and azaleas. If you just want to get out into nature, you may want to join the 20 million hikers and backpackers who put the national and state parks to good use each year.

Chances are you'll find a national, state, or local park in your area that offers scenic trails for hiking. Trail maps are often available to guide you; some show estimates of mileage and may indicate the degree of difficulty of the trails.

Even if you live in an urban area, you'll probably be able to find forest or wildlife preserves nearby that you can roam for a few hours. It's a healthy and inexpensive way to escape the noise and traffic of the city. It's also a good way to prepare your body for lengthier hikes across rougher terrain.

Your state board of tourism may be able to provide you with information about state and local parks. Local chapters of hiking groups and environmental organizations may also be able to assist you. To find out more about national parks in your area, contact the National Park Service (see Appendix A).

PREPARING YOURSELF

Before you head out on the wilderness trail, you'll need to prepare yourself for the greater intensity of hiking. Once you've completed the Starter and Basic Walking Programs in Chapter 5, you should be able to walk comfortably on level ground for four or five miles at a time.

Rarely will you find a hiking path that's smooth and level. So you'll need to condition your body for tackling hilly terrain. To do this, choose a four- or five-mile route near your home that has plenty of inclines. Since walking up and down inclines takes more energy than walking on level ground, you may have to begin at a pace that's slightly slower than your usual walking speed. Walk the entire length of this route three or four times a week for several weeks, until you can manage it comfortably at a moderate pace.

Your next step is to practice walking on hilly terrain with weight on your back. Even if you'll be sticking to short day hikes, you'll probably need to carry a few things with you. So fill your hiking pack with items you're likely to take, including a filled canteen, a small first aid kit, a raincoat or poncho, a sweatshirt, and some snacks. Then walk that four- or five-mile hilly stretch a few times a week for several weeks.

Once you've completed this round of conditioning, you should be ready for a day hike. You'll need to successfully complete a few day hikes—and practice walking with a heavier pack—before you'll be ready for an overnight trip. For your first hike, choose a well-marked trail that you can cover at a moderate pace in less than a day.

As you hike, choose a comfortable pace. You'll be walking for several hours, so don't race through the first mile. Be sure to give yourself rest stops, too. You may want to try stopping for about ten minutes each hour. More frequent breaks may cause you to lose momentum. If you absolutely need to rest a little more often, however, by all means do.

WHAT TO WEAR

When you start out on a hike, it's better to be wearing too much than too little. You'll want to be prepared for the worst, even if the weather is beautiful when you begin. Of course, you probably don't need to carry your snow gear for a mid-July walk through low altitudes. You will, however, want to wear or carry clothes that will protect you from rain, winds, and a sudden drop in temperature.

Dress yourself in several thin layers. This way, you can strip off layers if you feel too warm. Choose a soft material that absorbs sweat (like cotton) for the layer next to your skin. For your outer layer, try a light, breathable windbreaker. Also, toss a sweatshirt into your pack.

Even if rain doesn't look likely, it's best to come equipped with rain gear. In wet weather, a wet hiker can become frostbitten and hypothermic, even if the temperature isn't all that low. (See Chapter 10 for tips on dressing for cold and wet weather.) Bring along a large, foldable poncho for protection.

You'll also need a sturdy, comfortable pair of hiking boots or walking shoes designed for off-road terrain. (For information on choosing hiking boots, see Chapter 14.) Be sure to break them in gradually by wearing them around the house before you take them on the road. Invest in a good pair of socks to protect your feet from blisters. Nicely padded Orlon socks or wool socks with nylon liners work well.

You can find out more about preparing yourself for all kinds of weather by reading Chapter

10. You'll also learn how to recognize and treat the symptoms of weather-related ailments such as heatstroke and frostbite.

WHAT TO CARRY

The first item on your list of things to carry is water, even if you're taking a short hike. It's all too easy to become dehydrated during a hike, especially in warm weather. So you'll need to drink plenty of water as you go, even if you don't feel particularly thirsty.

You can't count on finding drinkable water along your route, so you'll need to carry enough for your entire hike. If you're planning a short hike, you may be able to get away with one container or canteen of water. For longer hikes, try filling three or four containers so that you can distribute the weight evenly in your pack.

The next item on the list is food. Hiking takes a lot of energy—at least 300 calories an hour (more if you're hiking at a brisk pace or on rugged or uphill terrain). Even if you eat an extra large breakfast before you begin, you're likely to get hungry on the trail.

Because you'll probably have to carry all the food you'll need, try to choose foods that are nourishing yet low in weight and bulk—and easy to prepare in advance. Particularly in hot weather, avoid bringing perishable foods, such as milk products and raw meat, that can spoil easily. Sandwiches and snacks of nuts, dried fruits, and dry cereal are favorite choices. They'll provide you with the carbohydrates you need for energy. A variety of dehydrated foods are also available, but these require water to make them edible.

Another essential item is a small first aid kit. This kit should contain bandages or sterile pads and tape, antiseptic, and aspirin or another painkiller. In addition, you may want to carry a pocket knife or a small pair of scissors, matches, a small flashlight, biodegradable toilet paper, and a good sunscreen. You may also want to bring a compass along. If you have a map of the area, be sure to keep it handy.

To carry all these items, you'll need a pack. The type you choose depends on the length of the hikes you intend to take. If you plan on taking short hikes, a fanny pack or day pack should be large enough. If you go on overnight hikes, however, you'll need a backpack that's a little roomier.

Packs come in a variety of models, sizes, materials, and colors. Some have internal frames, others have external frames. To find a pack that's right for you, visit a sporting goods store or outdoor gear store that has knowledgeable salespeople. Discuss with them the type of hiking you'll be doing, the supplies you plan to carry, and the amount of money you're willing to spend.

Be sure, however, to try the pack on before you purchase it. You'll be the one carrying it around, so you'll want it to feel comfortable. The pack should conform to your back. It should also have adjustable, padded shoulder straps and an adjustable waist belt that will allow you to distribute the weight of the pack to your hips as well as to your shoulders.

Once you've taken several day hikes, you may want to try an overnight hiking or backpacking trip. For these trips, you'll need to carry more supplies, including extra food and water, a sleeping bag, a powerful flashlight, a change of clothes, and perhaps even a tent and a small camping stove. This collection of necessities can add up to a heavy load.

Government researchers have found that carrying more than 25 pounds of weight for long periods can do more harm than good by straining the shoulders, back, and knees. This research grew out of complaints from soldiers who had to carry heavy packs during long marches. So it may be best to limit the load you carry on a hiking trip to 25 pounds, if it's at all possible. To cut down on weight, try choosing nourishing foods that don't need to be cooked, so you won't have to carry cooking utensils. If you're purchasing a sleeping bag or tent, choose lightweight models.

SAFETY

Part of the pleasure of hiking is the opportunity it gives you to explore wild areas and experience the wonders of nature. Even if you're hiking a trail for the second time around, you'll discover many new sights and sounds. But you can prevent some unpleasant surprises by taking a few precautions on the trail.

As a general safety precaution, it's best to walk with a companion, especially on long treks. Before you venture out, it's also wise to let someone at home know where you're going, which trail you intend to follow, and when you intend to return.

When you're on the trail, avoid drinking water directly from springs, streams, or lakes. No matter how clean and clear it looks, the water may be contaminated with a host of parasites and bacteria introduced by people or animals upstream. Boiling the water for at least one minute may help destroy some of these organisms. Portable water treatment kits are also available to help you purify water in an emergency. However, the best way to avoid illness from contaminated water is to pack and carry your own drinking water.

Poisonous plants are another trailside hazard. To guard against getting rashes from poison ivy, poison oak, and poison sumac, wear clothing that covers as much exposed skin as possible, particularly on the feet and legs. Wear long pants, socks, and shoes or boots. When you return home from a hike, remove your hiking outfit and toss it in the washing machine. If you do develop a rash from one of these plants, try applying an over-the-counter remedy, such as calamine lotion, to relieve itching.

Don't panic if you've been bitten by a tick. Not all ticks carry Lyme disease—a tick-borne illness that can cause chills, fever, headache, and other serious complications. Generally, a tick must remain on the skin for 24 to 48 hours in order to transmit the organism that causes Lyme disease. If you remove a tick from your skin, save it in a small jar of alcohol, so that if a suspicious infection develops, the tick can be analyzed for Lyme disease. There is no need to see a doctor unless you notice any signs of swelling or redness around the bite (a sign of infection), a bull's-eye-shaped rash (often a symptom of Lyme disease), a fever, or a skin rash.

If you're going on an overnight trip in the wilderness, you can protect your food—and yourself—from wild animals by stringing your food up at night. Place all food, as well as toothpaste, lotion, and other pleasant-smelling items, in a corded bag or your pack. Then string the bundle up high between two trees.

If you'll be hiking in an area that isn't off-limits to hunters, be sure to wear something bright, especially during hunting season. Orange caps are very popular for this purpose and are available in waterproof and breathable materials.

Finally, before you head out, be sure to read Chapter 10 to find out how you can prevent conditions like heatstroke, frostbite, and dehydration while you're on the trail.

GREAT AMERICAN TRAILS

The United States has an abundance of trails that can challenge your hiking skills. One trail that has captured the hearts of hikers young and old is the Appalachian Trail. Stretching from Maine to Georgia, the Appalachian Trail was originally a path used by migrating Native Americans. It was this nation's first "interstate" and, after the Revolution, it was maintained by the individual states through which it cut its swath. As vigorous a walk as it may seem to be, it has been conquered by a tremendous number of avid walkers.

Another great American trail is the Florida Trail, which acquaints walkers with Florida's wild side. The trail will be over 1,300 miles long when it is completed. It stretches from the Big Cypress Swamp in the southwest part of the state (near Naples), through Wekiva Springs and Ocala National Forest in the center of the state, to Blackwater State Forest in the northwest portion of the state (near Pensacola). For information on the Florida Trail Association, which maintains the trail, see Appendix A.

CHAPTER 8

STRETCHES AND
STRENGTHENERS

You can't count on any one type of exercise to make every part of your body
physically fit. Every athlete knows that
swimming, cycling, or yoga are only part of
a total exercise program. Swimmers and
cyclists may need to tone abdominals; people who practice yoga may need to concentrate on improving cardiovascular strength.

To improve flexibility and upper body
strength, walkers also need to round out
their walking program. In this chapter,
we'll show you how to lower your risk of
injury by increasing your overall fitness.

FLEXIBILITY

Walking will not help you maintain or improve
your flexibility (although it will enable arthritics
to keep their affected joints flexible). In fact,
walking may even reduce flexibility. Indeed, a

popular complaint among walkers is that before they began their walking program, they could touch their toes. After six months of walking, they can't. That's because walking causes the muscles in the back of the legs to contract. Repeated contractions shorten these muscles, tendons, and ligaments.

Lack of flexibility can be a serious problem, setting you up for a variety of painful injuries. To maintain your flexibility and ward off injury, you need to stretch your muscles before you put them to work. Stretching, both before and after your walks, is absolutely essential. If you skip stretching to save time, you'll probably end up losing time in the end as you wait for your sore and injured muscles to heal.

UPPER BODY STRENGTH

Though good for cardiovascular fitness, weight control, and attractive legs, walking does little for the muscles of the upper body. While it will help you lose weight without losing desirable lean body tissue, walking really won't build huge biceps or greatly strengthen your arms, neck, shoulders, and abdomen.

Round out your walking program and give your upper body a boost by using weights in your workout. You can visit a local gymnasium or health club and use weights or weight machines to strengthen muscles throughout your body. You can even incorporate simple strengthening exercises into your walking program. These exercises don't require expensive equipment or loads of spare time. They can even be sandwiched between your walks and your stretches.

STRETCHING AND STRENGTHENING

On the following pages, you'll find a series of stretches that you should perform before and after each of your walking workouts. Before you begin stretching, warm up your muscles by walking slowly for a few minutes (you may try walking in or around your home). Then stop walking and begin stretching. The exercises will loosen up your muscles.

End your walks with a cool-down period of slow walking and a repeat of your stretching routine. (Your muscles will be loose, so you'll be able to stretch them further.) By stretching after your workout, as well as before, you'll be able to improve your overall flexibility.

When you stretch, use a slow, smooth movement. Avoid bouncing, since this will cause the muscles to tighten. Stretch as far as you can, but don't stretch to the point of pain.

At the end of this chapter, you'll find several exercises that will help you strengthen your muscles, especially those in the upper part of your body. Do these strengthening exercises after your walk, but before you begin your cool-down stretches.

For both stretching and strengthening exercises, start out performing several repetitions of each exercise. Gradually build up to 15 repetitions per set and perform two to three sets of each exercise per session.

STRETCHES

Standing Calf Stretch

Stand straight with your feet shoulder-width apart. Step backward about 2 to 3 feet with your right foot. Keep your right leg straight, with your heel on the ground and your toes pointed straight ahead. Slightly bend the left leg forward. Support your upper body by placing your hands on your left thigh. Hold this position for 15–60 seconds. Repeat on other side, stepping backward with your left foot.

Standing Achilles Stretch

Stand straight with your feet shoulder-width apart. Step backward with your right foot, placing it about 12–18 inches behind your left foot. Keep your right heel on the ground and your toes pointed straight ahead. Bend your left (front) knee slightly. Sit back onto your right leg, letting the knee bend. Support your upper body by placing your hands on your left thigh. Hold this position for 15–60 seconds. Repeat on other side, stepping backward with your left foot.

Standing Quadriceps Stretch

Stand straight with your feet shoulder-width apart. Bend right knee, lifting right foot toward buttocks. Hold right foot with right hand. Stand upright, thighs parallel. Hold the position for 15–60 seconds. Repeat using left leg.

Standing Hamstring Stretch

Stand straight with your feet shoulder-width apart. Extend your right leg in front of you, with your heel on the ground and your toes pointing toward the ceiling. Bend your left knee. Lean forward at the waist, supporting your upper body by placing your hands on your upper left thigh. Hold for 15–60 seconds. Repeat on other side, extending your left leg in front of you.

Standing Chest Stretch

Stand straight with your feet shoulder-width apart. Reach behind your body with both arms and clasp your hands together, palms facing upward. Lift arms as high as possible without leaning forward at waist, squeezing shoulder blades together. This stretch should be performed slowly and smoothly. Hold 15–60 seconds. Repeat.

EXERCISES FOR STRENGTH

Push-ups

Regular Push-up: Keeping your body as straight as possible, flex the elbows, lowering your body until you almost touch the floor. Slowly raise yourself back up to the starting position. Repeat.

Modified Push-up: If you are unable to perform the regular push-up, decrease the resistance by supporting the lower body with the knees rather than the feet. (You can also try using an inclining plane, supporting your hands at a higher point than the floor, such as a table.)

Abdominal Curls

Lie on your back with knees bent and feet flat on floor. Choose from the following positions to vary the intensity:

○ Advanced—place hands behind ears

○ Intermediate—cross arms over chest

○ Beginner—place hands on top of thighs

Press your lower back into the floor. Raise your shoulders off the floor by contracting your abdominal muscles. Slowly lower your shoulders to starting position. Repeat.

Flies
(using free weights that weigh between 1 and 5 pounds)

Lying on a bench, hold dumbbells at arm's length above your chest. Keeping elbows slightly bent, lower arms in a wide arc to above chest level or until you feel a slight stretch in your chest. Lift arms in a wide arc back to starting position. Repeat.

Bent-Over Row
(using free weights that weigh between 5 and 10 pounds)

Stand to the left side of a bench. Place your right leg and hand on the bench in a kneeling position. Your left leg should be next to the bench, slightly bent, with your foot flat on the floor. Hold a dumbbell in your left hand with the left arm hanging down directly below the shoulder, palm facing toward the body. Pull the dumbbell to chest level, bending arm to 90 degrees, elbow stopping just above the shoulder. Slowly return to starting position. Repeat. Switch sides, placing your left leg and left hand on the bench and holding the dumbbell in your right hand.

Lateral Raises
(using free weights that weigh between 1 and 5 pounds)

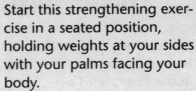

Start this strengthening exercise in a seated position, holding weights at your sides with your palms facing your body.

Slowly raise your arms up and to the side until parallel to the floor. Lower slowly to starting position. Repeat.

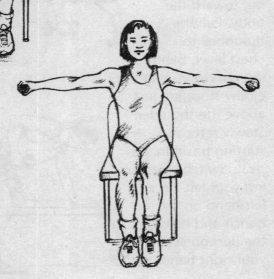

CHAPTER 9

COPING WITH PAIN

We've said repeatedly that a well-designed walking program should enable you to enjoy the benefits of aerobic training without injury. However, no matter how carefully you follow the Consumer Guide® Walking Program, you'll probably experience a few little aches and pains—simply because you'll be asking your body to do things that it might not have done for years.

We have included this chapter on coping with pain because we don't want a few minor physical discomforts to discourage you from continuing your walking program. You will undoubtedly gather your own little private collection of twinges and throbs that may be completely new to you. You are the best judge of what they mean, so pay attention to them. Pain is one way your body has of communicating with you. Most of the time, your pain will be caused by improper walking technique; improper shoes or socks; walking surfaces that are too hard; or too much walking, too soon. If you can't pinpoint the cause of your pain, talk with your doctor.

The ironic thing about aerobic exercises is that those organs we mainly want to exercise for the aerobic training effect—the heart and lungs—aren't the chief source of most of our discomfort. Instead, it's the feet, ankles, and legs—which have to work so hard to exercise the heart and lungs—that get into the most trouble.

To help prevent injuries and keep your walking pain to a minimum, you should do three things: Take good care of your feet; strengthen the muscles in your feet, legs, and abdomen; and develop flexibility throughout your body. Conditioning of the muscles in your lower body will take place naturally and automatically as you walk. But you can help your muscles along by supplementing your walking with calisthenics or other activities that help you build strength. To maintain and develop flexibility, however, you'll need to include plenty of stretches in your walking routine.

FROM THE GROUND UP

What follows is a brisk summary of the types of aches and pains that walkers may experience, from injuries of the feet to tightness in the chest. (It's important to note that people suffering from diabetes or circulatory problems should consult their doctor before embarking on a walking program. These individuals are particularly prone to ailments of the feet, and the consequences of even a minor cut, bruise, or blister can be severe.)

The toes. If you begin a walking program wearing shoes that are long on fashion and short on comfort, your toes will almost certainly let you know what a mistake you've made. Most toe discomfort results from poorly fitting shoes.

The length, width, and shape of your feet can—and do—change. With age, the ball of the foot tends to widen and the toes tend to spread. Therefore, you should have your feet measured each time you shop for shoes.

The size marked on a shoe doesn't really tell you whether it will fit your foot. Some manufacturers' sizes run large, while others run small. Select a design that matches the general shape of your foot as closely as possible. One way to do this is to trace your feet on a sheet of paper. Then, when you go to the store, compare your tracing to the bottoms of various shoes.

When you try on a pair of walking shoes, be sure they fit well in the toe area, too. One of your feet is probably larger than the other, and that bigger foot is the one you'll want to fit. Ideally, there will be a half-inch space between the end of the longest toe of your bigger foot and the inside end of the shoe. Each shoe's "toe box" (the part of the shoe that cradles the toes) should be high, long, and wide enough to accommodate your toes comfortably. (See Chapter 14 for more information on walking shoes.)

Corns. Corns are small, round mounds of dead skin caused by friction. Hard corns, the most common type, are dry and found most often on the outside of the smallest toe or on top of the other toes; soft corns are moist and usually appear between the toes.

In some cases, you can relieve corns by opting for shoes with softer uppers and toe boxes that are wider, longer, and higher. Cushioned pads or insoles can also offer relief by shifting pressure away from corns. If these efforts do not provide relief, see a podiatrist. Never attempt to remove a corn yourself.

Ingrown toenails. Few things are more aggravating to a walker than ingrown toenails. Ingrown toenails are nails, usually of the big toe, that curve inward along the edges of the nail bed, causing pain, redness, swelling, and even bacterial infection.

To prevent ingrown toenails, you need to keep your toenails trimmed. However, be careful not to taper the nails or trim them too short in the corners. Instead, trim the toenails straight across with a nail clipper.

Ingrown toenails can be aggravated by toe boxes that are too tight, so switching to a shoe with a wider toe box may help to relieve discomfort. Soaking the affected toe in warm, soapy water may also provide temporary relief. If the area around the ingrown toenail is severely swollen and painful, see your podiatrist.

Bunions. A bunion is a deformity of the big toe joint in which the joint juts outward and the big toe angles inward toward the other toes. Although the tendency to develop this condition can be inherited, wearing pointy, high-heeled shoes or shoes that are too tight in the toe area can aggravate the condition. As the joint becomes more inflamed, the bunion grows and becomes more swollen, tender, and painful.

A podiatrist may begin treatment by having you wear wider shoes and by prescribing a custom-made shoe insert called an *orthotic* (also known as an *orthosis*). The orthotic is made to compensate for the abnormality in the foot's shape and to shift weight away from the problem area.

If the bunion is already very large and painful, and if it interferes with walking, then surgery is frequently the only way to relieve the problem. In bunion surgery, the toe joint is realigned and excess bone may be removed.

Hammertoes. Hammertoe is a deformity in which a toe (or toes) hooks downward like a claw. Although the tendency to develop this condition can be inherited, high heels or shoes that fit too tightly in the toe area can also cause the condition. If the toe is severely hooked and painful and interferes with walking, your physician may prescribe an orthotic to reposition your toe properly. A corrective surgical procedure can also be used to treat some cases.

Neuromas. A neuroma is an abnormal collection of nerves that becomes irritated and inflamed. Neuromas occur between the bases of two toes, usually the third and fourth ones. Again, tight-fitting shoes can aggravate this condition. Neuromas can cause stabbing pain or a numb sensation. Soaking in warm water may help relieve the discomfort. Your doctor may prescribe an arch support or a special pad that can be placed inside your shoe to spread the nerve-pinching toes apart. Surgery to remove the neuroma can also be preformed.

Metatarsal stress fractures. The metatarsals are the long bones in your feet that are attached to the base of your toes. From the stress of walking, the metatarsals can develop fractures so small that they may not even be visible on an X ray. Often, they don't have to be splinted or put into a cast; they simply heal by themselves. But healing takes time, sometimes a month or two, and you'll probably have to suspend your walking program until this healing process is complete.

Blisters. These pockets of clear fluid or blood are common ailments. Regardless of the type of shoe worn and the protective measures taken, foot blisters continue to pose a problem for many people. They become a major problem only when they are severe enough to affect the quantity and quality of walking or when they become infected.

Foot blisters are caused by friction. The best way to prevent blisters is to prevent the friction that causes them. Here are some recommendations:

1. Buy high-quality shoes and make sure they fit properly.

2. Take good care of your shoes. Don't allow them to get brittle and stiff.

3. Break in new shoes before walking very far. A good idea is first to wear the shoes around the house for a few minutes each day. As they begin to soften, wear them for walking short distances. Try buying new shoes before your old ones wear out completely, so you won't be tempted to rush the break-in process.

4. Wear socks to help prevent blisters. The socks should be clean and should fit snugly. If they are too big, they can bunch up and cause friction. Ideally, the socks should not have seams in the foot area.

When a blister does develop, you can prevent infection by keeping the area clean. Do not puncture blisters. Leave them alone; bit by bit, they'll drain internally. If a blister ruptures, do not remove the skin; it serves as a protective covering. After a gentle cleaning with soap and water, place a pad of gauze over the open blister. Resting the foot will aid healing. Consult your doctor or podiatrist at the first sign of infection, such as redness or pus. If you are diabetic or have circulatory problems, consult your doctor at the first sign of a blister, no matter how small.

Calluses. A callus is a thickening of the skin that results from pressure or friction. A moderate amount of callus formation is normal; it's one way the foot protects itself. But when thick, hard calluses form, they can be painful. To help relieve pain, try switching to a shoe with softer uppers and a roomier toe box. Cushioned pads or insoles, and orthotics, can help. A simple scraping of the calluses by a podiatrist can also yield dramatic pain relief. Never try cutting calluses off yourself.

Walker's heel. This is a term some people use to describe a group of heel problems that include bone bruises and heel spurs. The syndrome usually starts with pain at the base of the heel—called *plantar fasciitis,* which involves inflammation of the tissues that attach to the bottom of the heel bone. Bone spurs are painful bony growths on the bone itself. These ailments may be worsened by walking on a hard surface, stepping on sharp objects, or walking in poorly designed shoes. These conditions don't lend themselves to a quick cure. Rest can be helpful, but not always convenient for the person who wants to maintain his or her aerobic conditioning.

A heel "donut" is often used to treat problems of the heel. This remedy is nothing more than a foam pad with a hole cut in it. The foam pad is taped over the bone spur, with the sensitive spot protruding through the hole.

Other modes of treatment include strapping the foot with an athletic bandage or switching to a shoe that has a springy rubber sole and a slightly higher heel. (This style of shoe helps shift the pressure of walking from the heel to the ball of the foot.) Soaking your feet in warm water can help relieve pain. If these measures don't work for you, see your physician or a podiatrist.

Achilles tendon injuries. The Achilles tendon is the thick tendon at the back of the leg that connects the heel and foot to the back of the calf muscles. It controls the hingelike action of the ankle.

Experts in sports medicine have identified three types of problems with the Achilles tendon. The first is *tendonitis,* which is an inflammation of the tendon. The second is a *partial rupture,* which is a tearing of some of the tendon fibers. The third is a *complete rupture,* or a complete break, of the tendon itself. The last two are not common to walkers, because walking seldom puts enough stress on the tendon to actually tear it.

Tendonitis can be caused by a sudden change in routine, such as walking on a level surface and then abruptly switching to sharp inclines or walking short distances and then taking a long hike. Symptoms of tendonitis are pain and stiffness an hour or so following activity, tenderness, and slight swelling. Tendonitis makes walking very difficult and painful.

Tendons can become inflamed as a result of ill-fitting shoes. The heels may be too low or too hard, the backs may be so tight that they strain the tendon, or the arch support in the shoes may not be supplying adequate support. Choosing a walking shoe with a slightly higher heel or inserting a sponge pad in the heel section of your shoes can help prevent the pain of Achilles tendonitis and of heel spurs, according to Charles Gudas, D.P.M, professor of orthopedic surgery and rehabilitative medicine at the University of Chicago Medical Center.

The very act of walking often tightens the tendons even more. To prevent Achilles tendonitis from developing, make sure that you do plenty of stretching when warming up and when cooling down. Stretching exercises can limber up the tendons and counteract the tightening effects of walking. Suggested stretching exercises include standing on the heels of the feet and drawing your toes up as far as possible or standing with your toes on a step and stretching your heels downward. Another good idea is to walk barefoot whenever possible—preferably indoors, so you won't have to worry about stepping on sharp objects.

Self-treatment of tendonitis is summarized by the acronym RICE—rest, ice, compression, and elevation. If it hurts, stop the activity and rest. Place ice or a cold compress on the affected area. Then wrap it in a flexible bandage (not too tight) and sit or lie down with your leg elevated. Remember, pain is a message that your body is sending to you. Don't ignore it.

Shinsplints. If you have shinsplints, you will feel pain in front of the lower leg when you put weight on your foot. You'll probably also find that your shin is tender to the touch. When you run your fingers along the shin, you may feel a roughened area along the bone.

Although the name implies damage to the shin bone, shinsplints may actually be caused by a variety of problems, including a muscle imbalance; improper body mechanics while walking; a hairline fracture of one of the bones in the lower leg; a muscle spasm caused by swelling of the muscle in the front of the leg; an inflamed or torn tendon in the lower leg; or irritation of the membrane between the two bones of the lower leg.

You can help prevent shinsplints by choosing your footwear and walking surfaces carefully. Sturdy shoes with cushioned soles are a must. If possible, switch from a hard walking surface to a soft one. (At a golf course or local park you can work out on the grass, which is much softer than pavement or track.) You may also want to put a sponge heel pad in the heel section of your shoe to help absorb some of the stress from walking on harder surfaces. If you walk on a track, vary the direction of your walks. In other words, instead of always going clockwise, walk counterclockwise on alternate days so that you're not always placing stress on the inside of the same leg.

Walking does a great deal to strengthen the muscles in the back of the leg, but it does less for those in the front. As a result, a muscle imbalance can occur. To compensate, you'll want to strengthen the muscles in the front. Flexing your foot up and down while wearing weights can help. If you don't have weights to strap onto your feet, sit with your legs dangling, feet not touching the floor, and have a friend hold your feet while you try to pull your toes up. Do this for three sets of ten each day.

The knee. The two main bones that come together at the knee joint are the thighbone and the shinbone. Usually, knee pains are associated with the kneecap—beneath it or along its sides. Sometimes the kneecap doesn't move smoothly against the lower end of the thighbone as it should, and the knee becomes increasingly irritated and swollen as you walk. If you have this problem, you may have to limit your walking. But first experiment with different walking methods. Many doctors think knee problems may be caused or aggravated by the way your foot strikes the ground when you walk. (If you walk indoors on a banked track in one direction for long distances, say 20 to 25 laps, your knees may be headed for trouble. Even subtle slopes can cause knee problems.) Many walkers and runners develop a painful affliction called runner's knee, in which the kneecap moves from side to side with each step. Runner's knee is most often caused when a foot collapses inward during walking (or running). When the foot collapses, the lower leg rotates inward and the kneecap moves to the inside. Repeated foot strikes will adversely affect the knee. Treatment usually consists of inserting orthotics in the shoes. It's also important for the walker to do leg exercises to strengthen and stretch the muscles on the front of the thighs.

Muscle cramps and spasms. A muscle cramp is an involuntary, powerful, and painful contraction of a muscle. The contraction may occur at any time—at rest as well as during activity. Cramps usually happen without warning.

Muscle cramps can be caused by fatigue; cold; imbalance of salt, potassium, and water levels in the body; poor blood circulation to the muscles; a sharp blow; and overstretching of unconditioned muscles. You may be able to reduce the odds of getting a muscle cramp by eating a well-balanced diet, by drinking plenty of fluids, by making sure you warm up properly before vigorous exercise, and by stopping activity before you become overly tired.

Once a cramp does occur, you can usually stop it by gently stretching the affected muscle. For instance, to relieve a cramp in your calf muscle, get hold of the toes and ball of your foot and pull them toward your kneecap. You may also want to try kneading the affected muscle firmly.

Usually, a sense of tightness or dull pain will follow a cramp. Applying heat or massaging the area may help relieve this discomfort. If you're plagued by frequent cramps, consult your doctor.

Sprains. Cramps and spasms are painful contractions of muscle tissue. In contrast, a sprain is a partial or complete rupture (tearing) of a muscle, tendon, or ligament, caused by overstretching. Small blood vessels in the area break, and pain develops when the surrounding tissue swells up and stimulates sensitive nerve endings.

To help prevent ankle sprains, you need to watch where you're going. Learn how to pick your way among the potholes and skillfully sidestep any debris in your path. If you do manage to sprain your ankle, you'll have to suspend your walking program until it is healed. Again, RICE (see page 128) will help bring down the swelling.

Muscle soreness and stiffness. Even people who have been serious walkers for years complain of some degree of regular soreness and stiffness. The pain is referred to as Delayed

Onset Muscle Soreness, or DOMS, and it usually occurs within 24 to 48 hours of physical activity. Often the discomfort lasts for only a few days.

For walkers, the most commonly affected muscles are the calf muscles and front and back muscles of the thigh. DOMS may be the result of small muscle tears and the subsequent inflammation that occurs in the muscle tissue. Taking anti-inflammatory medication or treating the affected area with ice may help control some of the pain.

It is practically impossible to completely avoid muscle soreness and stiffness. But you can reduce the intensity of the discomfort by planning your walking program so that you progress gradually, especially during the early stages. A slow, steady approach will allow the muscles of the body to adapt themselves to the stress placed upon them. If you become sore and stiff from physical activity, do some additional light exercises. Cooling down at the end of each and every workout and massaging the affected areas can also help.

Back pains. Lower-back pain can signal a slipped or damaged spinal disc. Some lower back pains result from exercising after years of relative inactivity. You will have to guess at the seriousness of these pains by the way you feel at the time; that is, by how intense they are, how disabling they are, and so on. If you have any doubts, however, see your doctor.

Couches and recliners can feel very comfortable; however, very few are designed with the health of your back in mind. Poor posture, such as slouched sitting, can place a great deal of stress on your muscles, ligaments, and discs. This stress can make it more difficult for proper healing to occur and may increase back pain. Choose postures and positions that allow you to keep the curves of your back aligned.

Many backaches are caused by mattresses that are too soft. In most cases, however, placing plywood beneath a soft mattress will not help. (Your spine won't get adequate support because there is still too much soft material between the plywood and your body.) What you should consider instead is a good orthopedically designed box spring and mattress.

Often, however, the cause of back pain is poor fitness—specifically, weak abdominal muscles. At the pelvis, the weight of the upper body is transferred to the lower limbs. The pelvis, or pelvic girdle, is balanced on the rounded heads of the thighbones. It is held in place by numerous muscles, including the abdominals, the hamstrings, the gluteals, and the hip flex-ors. An imbalance or weakness in these mus-cles can lead to pelvic misalignment, which usually causes the pelvis to tilt forward or backward.

If the abdominal muscles are weak, the top of the pelvis will drop and tilt forward. Forward tilt of the pelvis leads to *lordosis*, or sway back.

In addition to abdominal weakness, a lack of strength in the gluteals and hamstrings can lead to forward pelvic tilt. While the abdomi-nals stabilize the pelvis by pulling upward on the front, the gluteals and hamstrings offer sta-bility by pulling down on the rear of the pelvis.

Exercises must be done to strengthen the ab-dominals and gluteals. Usually, walking gives the gluteals a good workout. But the abdomi-nal muscles must be conditioned in other ways, such as through weight training or calis-thenics (see Chapter 8 for exercises you can do to strengthen your abdominal muscles).

If you have back trouble, or if you experience back pain when you walk, consult your doctor before beginning or continuing your walking program.

Side stitch. Side stitch goes by many names. It can be called a pain in the side, a stitch in the side, or a side ache. Sometimes it frightens people because it happens near the chest area. There appear to be two basic causes.

The first is improper breathing. This causes spasms in the diaphragm. To reduce this problem, "belly breathing" is suggested. That is, when you inhale, push your abdomen out. When you exhale, pull in your abdomen. It's just the reverse of what you normally do.

The second cause of side stitch is probably the most common. It's a stretching of the ligaments that attach themselves to the liver, pancreas, stomach, and intestines. These ligaments are put under stress when you walk vigorously. The bouncing action causes them to stretch, thereby causing pain.

One way to ease the discomfort of side stitch is simply to grip your side and push it in. You should also avoid eating a heavy meal within the three hours prior to the start of your walk. During the attack of side stitch, bend forward, inhale deeply, and push your belly out. If the pain is intolerable, see your doctor.

CHEST PAIN

Any pain in the chest, no matter what its cause, can be troubling—especially if you've reached middle age, when the risk of heart disease rises. Such pain may have nothing to do with your heart, however.

We are warned so often about heart disease that the slightest twinge in the chest area can conjure up frightening visions of permanent disability, or even death. A seizure in the chest can be, and often is, caused by cardiovascular disease. But more often it is caused by a simpler and less threatening ailment, such as heartburn or a strained muscle. In this section, we'll explain some of the possible causes of chest pain. (Any chest pain or discomfort, no matter how minor, however, should be brought to the attention of your doctor.)

Muscular causes

Chest pain or discomfort can be caused by a muscle spasm. A pulled pectoral (chest muscle) or a strained intracostal (side muscle) can cause a great deal of pain. A pulled muscle produces pain that is felt near the surface, and movements such as swinging the arm across the chest can initiate or worsen the pain.

Bruised muscles and ligaments may cause pain during deep breathing. Pressure during sleep from a hand, mattress button, or even a wrinkled sheet may aggravate bruised muscles. Pain associated with this kind of condition usually happens only during a certain motion or when pressure is applied to the area. Rest and time are usually the best treatments. Consult your doctor to be sure.

Heartburn

The pain brought on by indigestion, or heartburn, is frequently confused with pain caused by heart trouble. But this pain has nothing to do with the heart. Acid from the stomach backs up into the esophageal tube, causing contractions of the circular muscle of the esophagus. Milk or antacids may provide temporary relief, but a simple, well-balanced diet is the best prevention.

Angina pectoris

This type of chest pain or discomfort can occur when you're at rest, but it often develops during exercise or after a heavy meal. The condition is the result of a temporary failure of the coronary arteries to deliver enough oxygenated blood to the heart muscle. Such a failure is usually the result of obstructions to coronary circulation.

Angina usually isn't a sharp pain; it is usually a sensation of heaviness, as if the chest were being squeezed or crushed. The discomfort often spreads to the left shoulder, arm, or hand, where it may be felt as numbness. It may also be felt in the neck, jaw, and teeth. Pain or discomfort may occur minutes, days, weeks, months, or even years apart.

Angina is a warning sign. Your heart is telling you to stop. The problem is that the heart is not getting enough blood, and therefore, not enough oxygen. If you experience any pain or discomfort resembling angina, report it to your doctor immediately. Your doctor will probably want you to be very specific about where and when the discomfort occurs so he or she can more fully understand your condition.

The other pains or discomfort associated with heart disease are varied, yet similar to angina. They may be sharp, mild, or numbing. If you experience any of these pains, particularly a heavy sensation in the chest or a pain that radiates up the neck or down the arm, contact your doctor immediately.

The following symptoms may signal a heart attack: an extreme heaviness in the center of your chest, as if there was an elephant sitting there; an extreme tightness, like a clenched fist inside the center of your chest; or a feeling of stuffiness (something like indigestion) high in your stomach or low in your throat. Whenever you have a symptom that resembles any one of these, get to your doctor.

You may have gone through a stress electrocardiogram before you started a walking program and passed it with flying colors. If so, your chances of experiencing these symptoms are relatively small. But don't become cocky. A stress electrocardiogram, like most tests, is not 100 percent reliable. In the final analysis, your body, not somebody else's electronic equipment, has the final word. So listen to it.

CHAPTER 10

WALK, WEATHER OR NOT

Some days, the weather's going to be ideal for walking—very light breeze, temperature around 60 degrees, not a cloud in sight. What do you do, however, when the snow starts to fall, a gale threatens to blow you off the path, or the heat makes you feel as if your shoes will melt? It may not sound too appealing to you now, but you can walk in all but the worst weather. If you make walking as much a part of your routine as eating or sleeping, you'll probably find yourself walking through rain, snow, and sleet—and enjoying every minute of it.

The secret to all-weather walking is to be prepared—with appropriate clothing and gear and the knowledge of when to back off. Temperature extremes can be more than uncomfortable; they can be dangerous and even fatal if you don't prepare yourself adequately. But with good preparation, you can keep on walking outdoors under all but the most extreme weather conditions.

TOO DARN HOT

No matter how fit you are, you need to be careful when you walk in hot weather—especially if the humidity is high. Even experienced athletes can fall victim to serious heat-related ailments if they don't take special precautions. You may simply have to stop walking outdoors and move your walking program inside, into an air-conditioned track, gym, or mall (see Chapter 11, Finding Room to Roam).

Your body's built-in cooling system helps it to maintain its normal temperature of approximately 98.6 degrees Fahrenheit when you're in a hot environment. The evaporation of sweat from the surface of your skin causes cooling. In addition, the blood vessels in your skin dilate (expand) to let more blood flow through them. (That's why your skin gets flushed from a hard workout.) As your blood circulates through the innermost region of your body, known as the body core, it heats up. When it reaches the blood vessels in the skin, the heat radiates outward.

This natural "air-conditioning" system isn't foolproof, however. If you don't replace the water that you lose through sweat, you can become dehydrated. Without adequate water, your sweating mechanism can't work effectively. In the extreme case, this mechanism can shut down completely.

High humidity coupled with warm temperatures can also greatly hamper your body's ability to stay cool. When it's humid, there's already so much moisture in the air that your sweat can't evaporate as quickly. (On the other hand, a breeze can help your body maintain proper temperature by aiding in the evaporation of sweat.) As a result, your body loses water as it pumps out sweat, yet your body temperature continues to rise.

Another important factor in how well your body deals with heat is acclimatization. Your body needs anywhere from four days to two weeks to make physiological adjustments that allow it to cope with extreme heat. As the body becomes acclimatized, it lowers its threshold for sweating—in other words, it switches on the sweating mechanism before body temperature rises too high. In addition, it produces more sweat and distributes the sweat more effectively over the skin surface to allow cooling. The body also directs more blood toward the surface of the skin so that heat from deep within the body core can radiate out of the body. If the body hasn't had time to make these adjustments, however, it may not be able to handle heat effectively.

If you overdo it in the heat, you can develop a series of problems. There are three major types of heat illness: heat cramps, heat exhaustion, and heatstroke. Heat cramps are the least serious and heatstroke is the most threatening. Their symptoms overlap, however, and if proper measures aren't taken at the first sign of heat injury, heat illness can progress to its most severe form.

Heat cramps are painful muscle spasms that occur during or after intense exercise. The spasms usually occur in the muscles that are being exercised and may be caused by the loss of water and salt through sweat. The body temperature is usually not elevated. Rest and replacement of fluids can usually help relieve heat cramps.

Heat exhaustion, also called *heat prostration,* is a common heat-related illness that occurs most often in people who are not acclimatized to hot weather. It sometimes occurs after excessive perspiration, coupled with inadequate consumption of water to replace lost liquids. Symptoms of heat exhaustion include weakness; dizziness; collapse; headache; weak, rapid pulse; cold, clammy skin; and dilated pupils. The victim of heat exhaustion usually has a near-normal body temperature and continues to sweat. If you experience any of these symptoms while walking in hot weather, move to a cool place, rest, and drink plenty of water.

Heatstroke, also called *sunstroke,* is the most serious heat-related illness and requires immediate medical attention. Heatstroke occurs when the body cannot get rid of heat fast enough. The body's cooling system is overwhelmed and simply breaks down. Sweating usually stops, the circulatory system is strained, and body temperature can rise to 106 degrees Fahrenheit or more. If immediate steps to cool the victim aren't taken, body temperature will continue to rise and death may occur. Symptoms of heatstroke include hot, dry skin; rapid pulse; high body temperature; headache; dizziness; abdominal cramps; and delirium. Often, however, the first visible sign of heatstroke is loss of consciousness. Immediate steps must be taken to decrease the victim's body temperature. The victim should be moved to a cool area and placed in an ice-water bath or covered with ice packs until medical treatment is available.

There are a variety of steps you can take to protect yourself from heat illness. The cornerstone of prevention is water. If you intend to exercise in hot weather, you need to drink plenty of water before, during, and after your walks. You should drink 2 or 3 cups of cold water about 10 to 20 minutes before you begin walking. During your walk, drink at least a couple more cups of cold water. When you finish walking, drink water again. Don't rely on thirst to tell you when to drink; it's not always an adequate guide to your body's need for fluid.

Another important preventive measure is to slow down your pace and intensity when the temperature is high, especially during the first few days of a hot spell. By walking for a shorter time at a lower intensity early on, you'll give your body a chance to adjust its cooling mechanism to the heat.

During hot weather, you should schedule your walking workouts for the coolest part of the day—early morning or evening. Avoid walking late in the morning or during the afternoon when the sun's rays are most powerful. Also, try walking in shaded areas, such as parks, forest preserves, and tree-lined streets. If there's a breeze, walk with the breeze at your back during the first half of your walk. Then, for the second half of your workout, when you're hot and sweaty, walk into the breeze.

Proper clothing can also help you beat the heat. In hot, humid weather, wear as little as you can. Choose breathable fabrics that will allow your sweat to evaporate. (Cotton is an acceptable choice because it absorbs perspiration and allows sweat to evaporate.) Wear lightweight shorts and a loose-fitting T-shirt or tank top, or try a fishnet vest that lets air in and out. Also, be sure to choose light colors that reflect the sun's rays. If chafing is a problem, spread a little petroleum jelly on your skin in the affected areas.

Many walkers wear jogging outfits, which are available in various materials and designs. If you want to wear a jogging suit, make sure to get one that is made of a porous material. In warm or hot weather, you don't want heat and moisture to be trapped; you want it to circulate and escape to keep your body cool. So your warm-weather walking outfit should be made of either cotton or a lightweight, porous synthetic fiber and it should fit loosely without getting in your way.

Whatever you do, shun rubber, plastic, or otherwise nonporous sweatsuits. They create a hot, humid environment and interfere with the evaporation of sweat. Wearing them makes you an easy target for dehydration, heat exhaustion, and heatstroke. In addition, it's a misperception that the more you sweat, the faster you'll slim down: You'll promptly regain that lost weight as soon as you rush to the water fountain.

When you dress for hot, sunny weather, don't forget to cover your head. The head is the first part of the body struck by the powerful rays of the sun. By protecting your head, you can help control your body temperature when you walk. A lightweight, light-colored cap can help reflect the sun's rays. You may even want to try soaking it in cold water before you put it on.

To protect your skin from the sun's burning rays and help ward off skin cancer, be sure to apply a strong sunscreen to all exposed areas of your skin. Choose a sunscreen with a Sun Protection Factor (SPF) of 15 or more. You may even want to try a waterproof sunscreen, since you'll be sweating quite a bit.

Perhaps your most important protection against heat illness is knowing when to slow down and when to get inside. Regardless of your physical condition, you need to take into account more than the temperature of the air. As mentioned earlier, humidity can greatly decrease your body's ability to maintain its normal temperature.

Humidity makes the temperature feel hotter than it actually is. The Heat Index chart on page 150 tells you the "apparent temperature"—how hot it feels to the average person—for various combinations of air temperature and relative humidity. For example, when the air temperature is 85 degrees Fahrenheit and the relative humidity is 75 percent, it actually feels like it's 95 degrees Fahrenheit outside. You can find out the air temperature and the humidity level on any given day from local weather forecasts.

When the apparent temperature is between 80 and 90 degrees Fahrenheit, you need to use caution when exercising outside. This is especially true if you are just starting a walking program; if you are obese; if you have any serious health problems; if you take medication; or if you are over age 50. Under these conditions, you may need to cut down the amount of time you spend walking to avoid heat illness.

When the apparent temperature reaches 90 to 105 degrees Fahrenheit, heat cramps, heat ex-

Air Temperature (°F)

Apparent Temperature (°F)

Relative Humidity (%)	70	75	80	85	90	95	100	105	110	115
0	64	69	73	78	83	87	91	95	99	103
5	64	69	74	79	84	88	93	97	102	107
10	65	70	75	80	85	90	95	100	105	111
15	65	71	76	81	86	91	97	102	108	115
20	66	72	77	82	87	93	99	105	112	120
25	66	72	77	83	88	94	101	109	117	127
30	67	73	78	84	90	96	104	113	123	135
35	67	73	79	85	91	98	107	118	130	143
40	68	74	79	86	93	101	110	123	137	151
45	68	74	80	87	95	104	115	129	143	
50	69	75	81	88	96	107	120	135	150	
55	69	75	81	89	98	110	126	142		
60	70	76	82	90	100	114	132	149		
65	70	76	83	91	102	119	138			
70	70	77	85	93	106	124	144			
75	70	77	86	95	109	130				
80	71	78	86	97	113	136				
85	71	78	87	99	117					
90	71	79	88	102	122					
95	71	79	89	105						
100	72	80	91	108						

haustion, and heatstroke are possible if you exercise intensely outdoors. You should decrease the intensity and length of your workouts, walk in a shaded area, and be sure to drink plenty of fluids.

When the apparent temperature exceeds 105 degrees Fahrenheit, exercising outdoors is dangerous. Heat cramps, heat exhaustion, and even heatstroke are likely. Move your walking program indoors.

If you take care of your body's needs, it is possible—and safe—to walk in hot weather, even in Atlanta in August. But can you go for a stroll in Chicago in February?

WHEN IT'S COLD OUTSIDE

When the snow starts to fall and the temperature drops, it's easy to slip into inactivity and hibernate like a bear—but don't do it. Keeping up your walking program in winter will help you maintain your fitness level all year round. Getting out of the house can even help some individuals fight off the winter blues, known as *seasonal affective disorder* or *SAD*. So try to make it outdoors at least once a day for a walk. Be sure, however, to prepare yourself for the frigid temperatures before you step out the door.

Low temperatures and high winds pose the greatest threats to the cold-weather walker. The windchill factor tells you how cold the combination of low temperature and wind feels. Your own motion as you walk increases the windchill factor. If you don't protect yourself adequately from cold and wind, you run the risk of developing frostbite or hypothermia.

Frostbite is the partial freezing of a part of the body. Ice crystals can form within and between the cells in skin, tendons, muscles, and even bones. Frostbite is caused by overexposure to below-freezing temperatures. The extremities—hands, feet, ears, and face—are most vulnerable because your body decreases blood flow to these areas in order to keep your vital organs and muscles warm. These extremities are also the parts of the body most often left unprotected. The risk of frostbite is higher in heavy smokers, because nicotine causes constriction of blood vessels in the extremities. Without enough blood warming them, the hands and feet are easy targets for frostbite.

Signs of frostbite include pain and numbness, a white or blue discoloration of the skin, and loss of function in the affected area. Proper treatment of frostbite involves prompt, careful rewarming. The victim should be moved to a warm area, if possible. The frostbitten area should then be placed in lukewarm—not hot—water. Frostbitten skin should not be rubbed or massaged, as these actions can cause further damage to tissues. Contrary to popular belief, rubbing frostbitten skin with snow is not useful and can be damaging to the skin. Intense heat, from radiators, stoves, or hot water, should not be used because it may burn numbed skin.

Hypothermia is a condition in which body temperature falls well below the normal temperature of 98.6 degrees Fahrenheit. It's caused by prolonged exposure to cold. The first signs of hypothermia are severe shivering, slurred speech, and difficulty in walking. When body temperature falls below 90 degrees Fahrenheit, shivering usually stops and the patient may be confused or may lapse into unconsciousness. If emergency measures aren't taken to warm the victim, cardiac arrest and death may occur.

Basic treatment for hypothermia is rewarming of the victim. The rewarming must be done gradually to prevent the sudden enlargement of blood vessels at the surface of the body, which may divert too much blood from vital organs. Medical help should always be obtained for a person with hypothermia. While waiting for help to arrive, the victim should be moved to a warm place, covered with blankets, and, if alert, offered a warm, non-alcoholic beverage. Alcoholic beverages should not be given because they tend to reduce body heat.

You can avoid cold-related ailments by using caution when the temperature drops and the wind kicks up. Remember to dress in layers and wear a hat or other head covering. To avoid becoming overly fatigued, stop and take a break. Be prepared for emergencies and avoid drinking alcohol because it can contribute to dehydration and impair your judgement.

The accompanying Windchill Index chart tells you how cold it feels when both temperature (as shown on a thermometer) and wind speed are taken into account. For example, a thermometer reading of 30 degrees Fahrenheit combined with a 25 mile-per-hour wind is equivalent to a temperature of zero when the wind is calm. (The chart shows wind speeds up to 40 miles per hour only; wind speeds greater than 40 miles per hour have little additional affect on how cold it feels.) You can find out both temperature and wind speed from local weather forecasts.

Temperature/Actual Thermometer Reading (°F)

Wind Speed (mph)	40	35	30	25	20	15	10	5	0	-5	-10	-15	-20	-25	-30
Calm	40	35	30	25	20	15	10	5	0	-5	-10	-15	-20	-25	-30
5	37	33	27	21	16	12	6	1	-5	-11	-15	-20	-26	-31	-35
10	28	21	16	9	4	-2	-9	-15	-21	-27	-33	-38	-46	-52	-58
15	22	16	11	1	-5	-11	-18	-25	-36	-40	-45	-51	-58	-65	-70
20	18	12	3	-4	-10	-17	-25	-32	-39	-46	-53	-60	-67	-76	-81
25	16	7	0	-7	-15	-22	-29	-37	-44	-52	-59	-67	-74	-83	-89
30	13	5	-2	-11	-18	-26	-33	-41	-48	-56	-63	-70	-79	-87	-94
35	11	3	-4	-13	-20	-27	-35	-43	-49	-60	-67	-72	-82	-90	-98
40	10	1	-6	-15	-21	-29	-37	-45	-53	-62	-69	-76	-85	-94	-101

Little Danger

Danger

Great Danger

Windchill Factor/Equivalent Temperature (°F)

WINDCHILL INDEX

The "windchill factor" refers to how cold it feels when both temperature and wind speed are considered. The chart also shows you when exposed skin is in danger of freezing. If the windchill factor (equivalent temperature) falls in the section on the left, there is little danger for the properly clothed walker. The middle section shows that exposed skin is in danger of freezing. When the windchill factor falls in this range, you need to cover all exposed areas and watch carefully for signs of cold injury. If the windchill factor falls in the area at the far right, walk indoors.

When dressing for cold weather, simply reverse your hot-weather strategy. Instead of wearing light-colored clothing that reflects the sun's rays, choose dark-colored clothing that absorbs them. If you'll be walking in the evening or early morning, however, be sure to use reflective tape or a reflective vest so that motorists will be able to see you.

In addition, you need to construct a personal heating system that uses your body as the furnace. To do that, dress in layers of warm, loose-fitting clothing. The loose fit allows freedom of movement and promotes comfort. The layering strategy is very much like the insulation in your home; it keeps the heat in and the cold out. The layers of clothing trap warm air and hold it next to your body. The more you work, the warmer the air becomes. At the same time, these layers of warm air act as a barrier to the cold. When it comes to dressing for cold weather, it's the total thickness of the layers that really pays off.

The best choices for the innermost layer are polypropylene, silk, or thin, fine wool, because these materials "wick" the perspiration away from your skin. The middle layers should be made of knitted wool or synthetic pile. For the outer shell, use a windbreaker made of water-repellant, tightly woven material that "breathes." This breathable fabric will allow the water vapor from your perspiration to escape.

After a little practice, you will quickly learn what you'll need to wear for protection from the cold and wind. When you walk in cold weather, it is always better to wear too many layers rather than too few. That way, you can strip off layers, one by one, as your body heats up. You can then tie this extra clothing around your waist. Even better, however, try using an outer layer that has a zipper front. This way you can simply unzip the top layers to let the cool air in when you get too hot.

Be aware that, even in the winter, exercise can induce overheating. In warm weather, walkers tend to be on the lookout for signs of heat illness. By exercising continuously for over half an hour, you can raise your body temperature significantly, even if it's cold outside—but cold-weather walkers may not realize this. That's why you need to shed or unzip one or two outer layers as soon as you start feeling too warm.

It's even possible to get dehydrated in the winter, so it's important to drink plenty of fluids before, during, and after your winter walks. Cold acts as a diuretic, encouraging urination and fluid loss from the body. Out in the dry, cold air, you may lose more body fluid than you realize. Your thirst reflex is also depressed in the cold, so you shouldn't rely on it to tell you when to drink.

In addition to covering your body's core in layers of clothing, it is also important to protect your hands, feet, face, and head, which are most vulnerable to frostbite. Your feet are more susceptible to frostbite when they're wet as well as cold. You're also more likely to get blisters if your socks and shoes get soaked. In cold, wet weather, leather shoes are better than nylon or canvas ones, because they keep your feet drier. You can even put plastic bags over your socks. That may seem absurd, but it has enabled people to walk in snow with suede shoes for over 10 hours without ever getting their socks wet.

It's also important to wear socks when walking. Socks should be made of materials that absorb moisture well and allow adequate padding in the heel and ball of the foot. Some walkers prefer wearing Orlon sport socks or using liners with cotton or wool socks. Whatever your choice in socks, make sure your shoes are large enough to provide plenty of space around your toes. This space will fill with warm air that will insulate your feet nicely and ward off frostbite of the toes.

Some people like to wear two pairs of socks, especially in cold weather. That's fine as long as your walking shoes are big enough to accommodate the bulk of the extra sock. Otherwise, there won't be enough room for an insulating layer of warm air and you'll be more likely to develop a host of foot problems such as blisters and corns (see Chapter 9), in addition to frostbite. The inner pair of socks should be lighter in weight than the outer pair.

There are three basic lengths of socks: anklets that reach just above the shoe top, socks that go halfway up the calf, and knee socks. Knee socks and the calf-high variety are more suited for winter walking because they offer greater protection.

It has been estimated that a hat or cap can hold in 80 percent of the body's heat in cold weather. Without a hat, you lose more heat through your head than through any other part of your body. Put a cap on your head and, in effect, you've "capped" the heat's escape route. In other words, "If you want to keep your feet warm, wear a hat." You may want to try wearing a heavy knitted wool or Orlon ski cap that you can pull down over your ears and face. A mask can be a mixed blessing, however. Perspiration and condensation of the breath can freeze into ice around your mouth and nostrils—not the most pleasant winter experience. Some walkers have complained that a mask tends to congest the sinuses because it inhibits breathing. Nevertheless, for safety's sake, it may be a good idea to use a ski mask when the windchill factor is low.

When the weather is really nippy, make sure to keep your ears covered, because the ears are sensitive to low temperatures and can become frostbitten easily. If your hat doesn't cover your ears, try wearing a pair of earmuffs in addition to the hat.

Mittens, not gloves, give your hands the best protection in cold weather. Snuggled together in a mitten, your fingers help keep each other warm. Some people use tube socks as mittens, because they go well up the arm. In really cold weather, some walkers wear mittens with socks on top—or gloves covered by mittens.

Cold weather is no reason to pack away your sunscreen. It's true that sunlight is weaker in the winter, but the ultraviolet rays that burn skin and raise the risk of developing certain types of skin cancer are still a threat. When it is snowy and sunny, the reflected rays can burn your exposed skin, so it pays to apply sunscreen. If you use strong protection in the summer—that is, SPF 15 or higher—then use it in the winter, too. Alcohol-based sunscreens can add to the drying effects of the cold and wind and they don't stand up to perspiration as well as creamy ones do.

If you are driving to an out-of-the-way area to do your cold-weather walking, make sure you toss an extra set of warm clothing, a pair of shoes, and a blanket into the back seat of the car. This should be a regular emergency precaution—like the spare tire in the trunk. You might also want to bring a thermos filled with a hot beverage.

If you do venture out in extremely cold weather, particularly if you're planning a long walk, it is wise to arrange to go with a walking companion. It's also a good idea to let someone at home know where you plan to walk and what time you plan to return, especially if it's very cold or if it's snowing.

Just as it is dangerous to drink alcohol and drive, it can be dangerous to drink and walk—

especially in winter. The reason is that alcohol dilates the blood vessels in your extremities, redirecting blood away from your vital organs and toward your face, feet, and hands. This gives you a dangerous illusion of warmth, when in reality precious heat is being pulled from your vital organs. Alcohol also suppresses the natural shivering mechanism that helps generate heat. Like any other drug that impairs your judgment, alcohol can give you a false sense of well-being. You may literally forget when to come in from the cold.

COLD WEATHER AND HEALTH PROBLEMS

Cold weather shouldn't present any serious problems if you protect yourself and are in reasonably good health. If you have heart problems, however, ask your doctor if it is all right for you to brave cold weather—even if he or she has already given your walking program the go-ahead. The reason for this precaution is that the body's reactions to low temperatures put stress on the cardiovascular system. These reactions include constriction of blood vessels in the skin, shallow breathing through the mouth, and slight thickening of the blood, all of which can lead indirectly to angina (chest pain) in people with heart disease.

Cold lowers the heart's supply of blood, while exertion raises the demand for it. This imbalance between supply and demand can also cause attacks of chest pain. If you have heart trouble, your doctor can give you advice on how to minimize adverse effects of cold on your heart and when to do your walking indoors.

Even in people who don't have heart disease, cold exposure can raise blood pressure. To conserve heat, the muscles contract to obstruct the flow of blood to the arms and legs. This reroutes extra blood to the vital organs and boosts the blood pressure. People who have high blood pressure, therefore, need to take extra care in dressing warmly for cold-weather walks.

Asthma is another condition that can worsen in the winter. Inhaling cold, dry, winter air can trigger bronchospasms—contractions of the air passages in the lungs. To avoid this, many doctors advise their asthmatic patients to take their anti-asthma medications just before they exert themselves. If you have asthma, see your doctor before you walk in cold weather.

Also at special risk in the cold are people with Raynaud's disease, which often accompanies connective tissue diseases such as scleroderma and lupus. Cold causes spasms in their blood vessels, which cut off the circulation to their fingers and toes and turn their skin a "chalky" color. These people are advised to exercise indoors during cold weather.

OTHER WEATHER HAZARDS

Rain, snow, ice, hail, lightning, strong winds, fog, and other harsh weather conditions can curtail your outdoor walking. So can high altitudes and darkness. With a little bit of ingenuity, however, you may be able to walk your way around these hazards.

On warm days (temperatures above 70 degrees Fahrenheit), rain shouldn't be much of a problem as long as you keep your feet dry. On rainy days when the mercury dips below 70 degrees Fahrenheit, a light rain jacket will give you sufficient protection. The best materials are waterproof but breathable—that is, they don't let water in, but they do let out water vapor from perspiration. If you don't want to get your hair wet, you can either wear a hat or carry an umbrella.

Some people love to walk in the snow. To cope with the snow, simply follow the directions for walking in the cold (outlined earlier in this chapter). Be sure, however, to wear proper footwear to avoid slipping. Your pace will be slower, but that's okay. If the snow is deep, you'll be working just as hard as you would be at a faster pace on a clean street. If you doubt that, check your pulse.

Walking on the ice can be treacherous. It is easy to slip and injure yourself. If there is ice on the road or sidewalk, it's best to wait until later in the day, when it's been sanded, salted, or melted by the sun.

Hail can also be a problem. If the hail is large, take shelter immediately. If it's small, be your own judge. Most of the time, it won't harm you. As soon as you hear thunder or see any lightning, however, head indoors. Walking during a thunderstorm is dangerous.

If you're walking into a stiff breeze, you may want to slow down. Walking against the wind is like walking through deep snow. It takes extra work, so you'll get the same benefits that you would in a faster walk under normal circumstances.

High altitudes offer a source of special problems. At 5,000 feet above sea level and higher, the air contains significantly less oxygen than it does at lower altitudes. So there is less oxygen for your body to take in. As a result, your heart has to work extra hard. For every 2,500 feet that you ascend, plan on taking at least a week to adjust to the decline in oxygen concentration. One way that you might adjust is to cut the pace or duration of your program by 50 percent at the beginning. If you find yourself short of breath at that rate, slow down even further.

When the weather turns foggy, follow all the guidelines for walking in darkness (presented in Chapter 11), with one exception: Don't wear white, gray, or other light-colored clothes. Motorists will not be able to see you. Bright red or orange clothing is best.

CHAPTER 11

FINDING ROOM TO ROAM

One of walking's great advantages is that you can do it almost anywhere. To find a place to walk, all you have to do is step outside your door. By varying the paths you choose to take, however, you can make walking that much more pleasurable—and practical.

Regular, frequent walks provide an ideal opportunity to explore the area in which you live. Each walk can be an adventure, a chance to experience what's going on around you. Even brisk walking affords you a good look at the sights around you. You can see the seasons change—and treat yourself to all sorts of sights, sounds, and smells. Where you choose to walk is up to you. The range of choices is unlimited—at least as far as space is concerned.

Maybe you're lucky enough to live in an area, town, or city that offers not just walking space—every area has that—but different kinds of space to make your walks as interesting as possible.

COMPARISONS OF SURFACES

When you choose a route, pay close attention to the surface. A lot of walkers say grass or packed dirt is the very best surface for walking. These surfaces are soft, so they are good for shock absorption. Ideally, the surface should be smooth enough to allow you to walk as fast as you want without tripping or twisting an ankle. If the grass or dirt is too clumpy, it won't provide good enough traction and you may stumble or fall.

With a little exploration, you can usually find some strip of grass or other unpaved surface on which you can walk. Walking on a sandy beach is very enjoyable. You can even do it barefoot—but you need to watch out for sharp shells or other debris. Walking on soft sand or dirt can increase the energy you expend—and the calories you burn—by as much as one third. It also provides the muscles in the feet with more of a workout, particularly if you walk barefoot.

If you can't find a soft, springy surface to use, pavement is an alternative. One good thing about pavement is that you don't have to travel far to find it. But it does have its drawbacks. Most foot and leg problems are either caused or aggravated by walking on hard surfaces like concrete or asphalt. Wearing good, shock-absorbing walking shoes can help you avoid injury.

HILLS AND STAIRS

Walking up hills and stairs burns extra calories and raises your heart rate more than freestyle walking does at the same speed on a flat surface. Thus, it does an even better job of helping you control your weight and build your aerobic capacity. It also provides more of a workout for the large muscles in the buttocks and the muscles in the front of the thighs, which are responsible for lifting the legs, climbing, and pushing off.

With the heightened benefits of walking on hills and stairs comes an increase in your risk of injury. Some simple adjustments in your walking technique can help you hold down this risk. For instance, while walking uphill, walk slightly slower, lean forward, and swing your arms more vigorously to increase your climbing power. Downhill walking is even harder on the bones and joints, and its high impact forces can aggravate joint problems and cause muscle soreness. To minimize the shock, shorten the length of your stride.

If you have trouble finding stairs or hills that you can climb, you may be able to find an exercise machine called a *stair-climber* at a local gym or health club.

CITIES, SUBURBS, AND BEYOND

The ideal outdoor walking route is a course with a smooth, soft surface that doesn't intersect with traffic. For that reason, parks are excellent walking areas for urban dwellers. Parks usually offer soft surfaces like grass and packed dirt to walk on. In addition, they are often secluded from traffic's noise and toxic emissions. If it's allowed, you might also try walking along the perimeter of a local public golf course. You'll need to stay alert for stray golf balls, though.

There's another thing you can do to have an enjoyable walk, even if you're not surrounded by trees, grass, and fresh air. Find an old residential neighborhood with beautiful houses or historic buildings that can occupy your attention while you walk. Some historic areas even offer guided walking tours. Be sure that you don't get carried away by the sights, however, and neglect to watch where you're going.

If you walk in an urban area, try to stay away from traffic lights and congested areas. A lot of stop-and-go walking can cause you to lose momentum and break your stride. It can also decrease the aerobic benefits you get from your walks by allowing your heart rate to drop out of your target range. If your urban or sub-urban route is dotted with traffic lights, how-ever, don't just stand still when the light is red. Instead, try walking in place until it turns green and you can go forward again. This will keep your heart rate up while you wait.

If you live in a rural area, you'll have a wider selection of peaceful, grassy walking routes. Paths that border rivers and streams or encircle lakes can make pleasant walking routes, as long as they're not too muddy or slippery. If you follow a narrow rural road, however, you'll need to stay alert for ditches and fast-approaching vehicles. If you choose a field or hilly area, watch out for holes and other stum-bling blocks. Be sure to read the safety section at the end of this chapter, especially if you'll be walking in the evening or early morning when lack of light can be a hazard.

MALL WALKING

Some cities, endeavoring to bring their declining downtown areas back to life, have created outdoor walking malls by banning cars from certain shopping streets. These outdoor shopping malls give you the opportunity to window-shop or run errands while you walk—without having to worry about traffic. (Be careful not to stop walking too often or for too long, however, because you'll decrease the aerobic benefits of your walks.)

Even more common, though, are enclosed shopping malls that cater to walkers by lengthening their hours. Some even let walkers in before dawn or during holidays when all the stores are closed.

Many malls now have community-sponsored walking programs. Some have collaborated with local hospitals or health organizations to establish walkers' clubs that provide awards for walking certain distances, discounts for shopping at the mall, occasional free breakfasts, and mileage logs for members. Some malls even offer measured walking courses, so walkers can calculate precisely how far they've gone. Also available in some malls are walkers' maps, fitness seminars, health screening (for blood pressure, for instance), and special stations with instructions for stretching and calisthenic exercises.

Mall walking has many advantages. It gets you out of the house but protects you from the safety hazards, inconveniences, weather extremes, and air pollutants that you might have to struggle with if you did all your walking outdoors.

Malls tend to be conveniently located and safe. Their climates—temperature and humidity—tend to be controlled and kept in a comfortable range. Thus, malls play a major role in promoting all-weather fitness. They offer real protection from the possible adverse health effects of walking in extremely cold or hot weather, a concern particularly for people with heart disease.

Malls that have become popular spots for walkers offer yet another advantage. They turn walking into a sociable activity. Even if you arrive at the mall alone, you'll probably be able to meet other walkers there. Eventually, you may have a large group of walking companions, at least some of whom will be there each time you visit the mall. This kind of peer support can provide crucial motivation to keep you walking.

Of course, the advantages are reciprocal: Walkers don't just benefit from malls; malls glean benefits from walkers. Many mall managers realize that public services such as walking programs are a good way to get people to come to the mall. Walkers help increase mall traffic and frequently patronize mall stores. If you're interested in mall walking but can't find a mall near you that offers a program, you might try contacting a local mall manager to discuss these reciprocal benefits of setting up a program.

GYMNASIUMS AND HEALTH CLUBS

Many gymnasiums and health clubs feature indoor tracks, treadmills, and stair-climbers that you can use to move your walking program forward when poor weather or safety concerns force you to cancel your outdoor walk. This setting also offers you an excellent opportunity to integrate your walking program with weight training, aerobics, dance, swimming, and other physical activities.

INDOOR/OUTDOOR TRACKS

Walking around and around the same track can be boring. If you are trying to walk a mile, it may take you 20 or more laps. Your mind can grow numb, and it is easy to become discouraged. You can help fight this by walking with a companion, by varying your tempo lap by lap, or by mentally organizing your schedule or planning your day as you walk.

If you are going to walk on an indoor track for several days or more, it is best to switch directions. By walking clockwise one day and counterclockwise the next, you will help avoid orthopedic problems that can result from continually rounding corners in the same direction. Some clubs have even incorporated clockwise and counterclockwise days into their club's track schedule. This is particularly important if the track you're walking on is banked (slanted), because the leg on the down side will be subjected to extra stress.

TREADMILLS

Treadmills are not just for jogging. They are also good for walking. Essentially, a treadmill is a conveyor belt that is designed to allow you to walk or jog in a confined space. There are two kinds of treadmills: motorized and non-motorized.

Walking on a motorized treadmill is as close to real walking as you can get without actually hitting the street or track. You simulate your natural freestyle walk almost exactly. In motorized treadmills, an electric motor rotates the conveyor belt (sometimes called a *walking bed*) under your feet, forcing you to walk at a set speed (the speed can be adjusted). The walking bed of many motorized treadmills can be raised at one end to simulate walking uphill or downhill, making the exercise that much more difficult and thus increasing its aerobic value.

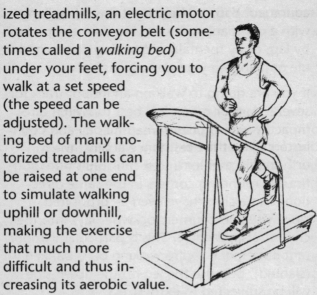

This is an especially useful feature for people who are in such good shape that they need to walk uphill to get their heart rates well into their target zones.

Perhaps most important, a motorized treadmill allows you to walk for precise distances at exactly measured speeds. This is particularly important if you need to monitor your fitness plan carefully or want to keep precise track of your speed. Motorized models have mechanisms that adjust speed in small increments—one-tenth of a mile or less—so that you don't have to jump from a gait that is much too slow to one that is far too fast.

When you walk on a nonmotorized treadmill, your legs do the work of rotating the walking bed. Compared to motorized treadmills, nonmotorized ones are usually lighter and more compact. Nonmotorized treadmills can also be adjusted so that the resistance against the running bed is higher, or lower, making the workout more, or less, strenuous. Unlike motorized treadmills, they do not allow precise predetermination of the speed at which the running bed rotates, so you may have some trouble keeping track of your pace from one workout to the next.

Walking on a nonmotorized treadmill also tends to be less comfortable than walking on a motorized one. When you use a motorized treadmill, your legs propel you forward just as in normal walking. When you walk on a nonmotorized model, on the other hand, your legs push the running bed backwards. Nonmotorized treadmills can be uncomfortable and difficult to work for the long periods recommended for aerobic conditioning—30 minutes or more. The belt is on rollers, and after a period of walking, exercisers may experience a "hot foot" because of the built-up friction.

Walking on a nonmotorized treadmill is fine if you're going at a slow to moderate pace, but it can lead to foot and leg irritation at faster paces. Nonmotorized treadmills are also generally built with an incline, which may be harmful to those with knee or hip problems.

Many gyms and health clubs have treadmills that you can use. Most motorized treadmills designed for home use cost over $2,000, with prices as high as $8,000 for some models. Nonmotorized treadmills are generally less expensive. Their prices start at about $500.

Regardless of which type you choose, a home treadmill is a sizable investment. So if you decide to purchase one, it's a good idea to try it out in the store before you make any purchase decisions. Walking beds vary in length from one model to another, so make sure the bed is long enough to accommodate your natural stride. The motor should have at least 1.5 horsepower. You should also inquire about the service history of the treadmill model you wish to purchase. Make sure your treadmill will be easy to maintain and repair if necessary.

SAFETY

As you discover new and different places to walk, always consider safety. Traffic must always be taken into consideration. Particularly if you have to walk directly on the street instead of on the sidewalk, you need to stay alert and watch out for vehicles. Even if you wear reflective strips on your clothing, you may not be seen by a motorist. So walk as you drive—defensively.

A special type of mask has been designed to filter the polluted air many people in urban areas must breathe. If you must walk near cars and trucks that spew out carbon monoxide and other noxious fumes, a mask of this type might make breathing easier.

Even when you have a nice trail available, and traffic isn't a problem, you may still have to look out for bicycles. Collisions can cause serious injuries.

In addition, some city areas are just not safe enough to walk through—certainly not after dark. The best way to protect yourself against these possible dangers is to avoid these areas. If you're planning on walking an unfamiliar route, you may want to drive through it first to check it out. If you find that you've walked into a dangerous area, try to carry your body aggressively, walking briskly and purposefully to an area where you will feel safer. Look like you know where you're going, even if you don't. A person who looks lost is an easy target of street crime.

There are also some things to watch out for if you plan to walk in the countryside. Make sure you're not trespassing. Also, be careful that you don't get carried away by the beauties of nature and the music of the birds—and get lost. Many adventurous walkers like to take along a pocket compass as a safety precaution.

Wherever you go, be sure to watch out for dogs—the well-known scourge of walkers, joggers, and mail carriers. If you encounter a dog, try not to look scared. Just back away from it slowly. Do not turn your back on the dog. If the dog looks as if it's going to charge at you, shout "down" or "no" in a stern, angry tone; this may help scare the dog off. If the dog does attack, lift your knee up to help protect your body and hit the dog in the snout with a stick, rock, or your arm. Call out for help. If you've been bitten by a dog, seek immediate medical care.

For safety's sake, if you listen to an audiocassette or radio as you walk, make sure to keep the volume low enough so you can hear what's going on around you. Because it is so easy to get carried away by the music, your attention to your surroundings may not be enough to keep you safe. Always be alert. Listen and watch for cars, bicycles, and other pedestrians, especially when you're turning a corner. When walking at night, follow these basic guidelines:

1. Face the traffic as you walk, and stay close to the edge of the road. If a car seems to be bearing down on you, stop walking and step off the road.

2. Wear light-colored clothes. White is best. You might also try wearing reflective tape or a reflective belt or vest.

3. Carry a flashlight so you can see where you're walking; the light will also alert motorists to your presence.

4. Try to avoid walking on any road at night before you've had a chance to get familiar with the road during the day. By checking out the road during daylight hours, you'll know where the curves and ditches are.

5. Don't look directly at the headlights of on-coming cars. They tend to blind you, and, as a result, you can't see where you are going. Instead, look off to the side. You'll still be able to see the car with your peripheral (side) vision.

CHAPTER 12

FINDING TIME
FOR FITNESS

You're convinced, right? We've succeeded in talking you into beginning a walking program and getting yourself into shape. You've explored new places to walk and found plenty of room to roam. You've checked up on your health, figured out your target heart rate, and chosen the walking program that's right for you. That's great.

However, if you're like many people with busy schedules who know they ought to be more active, you may already be wondering how long you'll be able to stay with your walking program. Maybe you're asking yourself: "How long will it be before I lose interest, am sidetracked by an extra-busy time at work, or invent any number of other excuses for not walking?"

Don't let these worries keep you from starting to walk. Begin now, and refer to this book whenever you feel the need for another dose of encouragement. In this chapter and the next, you'll find suggestions for sticking with your walking program. This chapter focuses on fitting fitness into your schedule—not only in terms of finding time to walk, but in terms of making regular walking a priority in your life.

THE DROPOUT PROBLEM

When it comes to getting health benefits from physical activity, your ability to stay with a regular exercise program for life is even more important than the intensity of the activity itself. Unfortunately, figuring out how to get people to take up exercise and integrate it into their lifestyles permanently hasn't proved all that easy for exercise scientists.

Nearly 50 percent of people who begin a supervised exercise program drop out within 6 months to a year, according to Rod K. Dishman, Ph.D., associate professor in the department of physical education and director of the Behavioral Fitness Laboratory at the University of Georgia, in Athens. The dropout rate is the same regardless of whether people exercise in community and work-site fitness programs, in programs to prevent first and second heart attacks, or in outpatient programs for the treatment of overweight, diabetes, or depression. In fact, many patients referred to an exercise program by their doctor or hospital never even show up for the first session.

Exercise demands more time and effort than do many other health-promoting behaviors, like brushing and flossing your teeth or having your blood pressure checked. The knowledge that exercise can provide health benefits may help people get motivated to begin an exercise program. However, their continued involvement over the long haul appears to depend much more on positive reinforcement from friends, family, and health professionals, and on a sense of personal well-being and achievement.

Instead of concentrating too much on official exercise programs, Dr. Dishman advises, more attention should be paid to motivating the estimated 65 percent of the American population who are currently sedentary. These are the people who stand to benefit most from adding more physical activity to their lives. These individuals are also more likely to begin and continue a less strenuous exercise program such as walking.

Studies of exercise compliance have identified convenience as a major factor. People who drop out of exercise programs tend to live farther away from the exercise site than do those who stick with it. Convenience is one reason why walking has such a low dropout rate as a lifelong exercise program. Walking really can be incorporated into your daily routine, no matter how crammed full of duties it is.

Compared with an exercise class at a health club, for instance, following your own personal walking program saves you both money and time. In addition, although you may enjoy walking with a friend or family member, walking is something you can do on your own as well. You can set your own walking schedule, without having to wait for your partner or team to show up, as you would have to do for many other activities.

BUILDING WALKING INTO YOUR LIFE

You can build walking into your life in a variety of ways. One convenient method is by turning everyday errands and chores into opportunities to walk. Taking your dog for a brisk, 30-minute walk, for instance, can provide both you and your pet with a hearty workout. If you need to take clothes to the dry cleaner, try choosing one that's a mile or two from your home and walk the distance instead of driving. If you have a baby at home, break out the baby carriage and go for a lengthy, moderately paced stroll that can lull your baby to sleep and give you an aerobic workout. You can even purchase a three-wheeled push cart that's designed for this purpose.

If you need to go to the shopping mall to pick up a few things, try parking at the far end of the lot and walking to the door—or better yet, choose a mall that's within walking distance and leave your car at home. Once you're inside, take a quick trip or two up and down the length of the mall before you begin shopping. After you've purchased everything that you need, take another couple of brisk laps around the mall.

If you work sitting at a desk for most of the day, try walking during your lunch hour, as well as to and from work. If you have to attend appointments outside of the office, use them as another chance to walk. Besides, such a work-day break can actually clear your head and buy you a little extra time to mentally prepare for a presentation.

Whether you work on the second floor or the tenth, try walking up the stairs instead of taking the elevator to your office. This can help tone the muscles in your legs and buttocks and help you burn calories even if you have only a couple of flights to climb. If you work on one of the top floors in a skyscraper, try getting off the elevator several floors before yours and take the stairs the rest of the way. Work-site studies have shown that workers who simply began using the staircases instead of elevators and escalators improved their overall physical fitness by 10 to 15 percent.

Even when you have to spend hours at your desk or computer terminal, you can practice an essential part of your walking fitness program. You can do stretches frequently throughout the day to maintain your flexibility. (The more flexible you are, the less chance you'll have of injuring yourself when walking.) Stretching can also help to relieve tension and give you an energy boost. And you don't need to change clothes or leave your work area to do many of these stretches. You can do head tilts, shoulder shrugs, leg lifts, and ankle twirls while you're seated. Then, when it comes time for a coffee or restroom break, you can stand up and stretch your legs. Visit a coffee machine or restroom that's on a different floor, so you can use the stairs to get there and back.

If you have to go on a business trip, there's no reason to suspend your walking program. If possible, ask your travel agent to book you into a hotel within walking distance of your appointments. If your travel plans include lengthy layovers at airports, pack your walking shoes and use the extra time to explore your surroundings.

The key to fitting fitness into your schedule is to not take the easy way out and succumb at every opportunity to every time-saving modern invention designed to keep us from walking. The subliminal message we get from being constantly surrounded by all these inventions is that walking is something we should avoid. But as this book explains, walking is actually good for you and worth incorporating into your life at every opportunity. So the next time you find yourself driving around the parking lot looking for that space up front, think about the benefits of walking. Then head to the far end of the lot, park your car, and take a walk.

THE WALKING COMMUTER

Many walkers have managed to work their walking program into their daily commute to and from work. These individuals are proof of what we've been saying throughout this book: Walking is the easiest of all exercises to build into your routine. Walking to and from work may take a little longer than commuting in a car, bus, or train, but the rewards are well worth it.

If you travel by public transportation for many miles to get to work each day, you might assume that there's no way you can walk to work. You can't walk the entire distance, that's true. If you take public transportation, on the other hand, you can try getting off the bus or train one or two stops early and walking the remaining distance.

If you drive to work, you might save money and time if you walk part of the way. As many long-distance commuters know only too well, the longest part of the drive to work is often the last mile or two, as you near the congested area that everyone is converging upon. If you're really unlucky, it can take the last ten minutes of an hour-long drive just to get through the last four blocks. If you parked your car four, six, or eight blocks from work, you could probably walk that distance in the same amount of time it takes you to drive, fight for a parking space, and get to your office. You might even beat your driving time by walking that last bit of the trip. Chances are you'll also pay less for parking, because you won't be fighting for a prime parking space. Depending on the location, if you play your cards right, you may even be able to find a free space.

CORPORATE PROGRAMS

Many corporations have taken up the idea of a corporate fitness program that stresses walking. Some of these programs involve a brisk two- to four-mile walk, with warm-up and cool-down sessions, during lunch hours. An increasing number of employers are realizing that they can make an important contribution to their employees' welfare and productivity simply by encouraging them, through financial and physical incentives, to walk to work, at least partway.

If your employer hasn't jumped on the bandwagon, you might try bringing up the idea. Here's one idea that deserves consideration: The company could rent parking lots a mile or two away from its offices, so employees could park there and walk to work. In case of bad weather, umbrellas could be placed at the office and parking lots for use by the walking employees. This system has the built-in potential for progress checks and rewards. Some sort of sign-in or sign-out procedure could be used to check whether employees use the facility. Many companies are already awarding their physically fit employees with special financial incentives.

Some company managers may read this suggestion and think, "Terrific. But how much is all this walking going to cost, and who's going to pay for it?" In a way, it would be just like any other investment. It might cost a few dollars at first, but that money would quickly pay dividends in terms of healthier, more productive employees who take fewer days off for illness. And it probably wouldn't hurt the company's insurance rates, either. In fact, employee fitness programs are not just an attractive fringe benefit but also a profitable investment for the company. Such programs have been shown to result in decreased absenteeism, reduced health care costs, and increased productivity.

Corporate leaders are realizing that a walking program can be the simplest and least expensive way to get their employees moving with regular exercise. And regular exercise has been shown to help employees escape everyday office pressures and competition—and become more productive at work.

WALKING ON THE JOB

There are some people who may not need to concentrate so hard on building walking into their commuting or their lunch hours. These are the ones for whom walking is actually an integral component of their daily work.

Examples include waiters, waitresses, ushers, meter readers, garbage collectors, caddies, mail carriers, and police officers on the beat. If you walk a lot on your job, pay attention to how often you stop. If you don't walk continuously, you may not be getting much of an aerobic training effect, so you may want to schedule regular, vigorous walks outside of work to improve your fitness level.

THE PROPER ATTITUDE

When you're trying to fit walking into your lifestyle, having the proper attitude can make all the difference in the world. After all, you're not as likely to find time to exercise if you look at it simply as a chore. In this section, you'll find some simple steps you can follow to make exercise a natural, convenient, and enjoyable part of your daily routine.

Step One: Set a goal. Goals are important in life. They give you something specific to work toward and a way to measure your progress. When you're setting a goal, avoid vague generalizations like these: "I want to get into shape," or "I want to lose weight." Instead, set precise long-term, intermediate, and short-term goals.

For instance, if you want to lose weight, decide how much weight you want to lose in six months or a year. If you want to lose 20 pounds during that period, that is your long-term goal. Your short-term goal might be three pounds by the end of the first month. (Your intermediate goal would be somewhere in between.) Ask your doctor for assistance in planning a healthy, realistic weight loss program.

What kind of goals should you set? What would you like to achieve? Whatever it is, write it down. Even if it seems unrealistic at this time, put it on a sheet of paper or a card and save it. This is your long-term goal. Once a week, you can take out the sheet of paper, write down your progress, and make a note of anything that seems to be preventing you from achieving your goal.

Next, you need to plan how you are going to reach your goals. Write down your plan, and be specific. For instance, how many additional minutes of walking are you going to do each week to accomplish your long-term goal?

Finally, make a note of what you'll do today—not tomorrow, but today. Write down how long, at what time, and where you're going to walk.

Step Two: Record your progress. For some people, the thing that makes sports like football, basketball, and baseball so endlessly fascinating is the competition. If competition really gets you moving, you can get it from race-walking—or even from competing against yourself. Just use a progress chart to record how well you're doing and how close you're coming to your goal. Charting your progress can give you the sense of achievement that helps keep many exercisers motivated. And the chart doesn't have to be complicated. The simplest chart is just a regular calendar on which you write the information about your walking progress.

Many people record their mileage on a map. Your regular walking route may take you around the same section of your neighborhood every day, but you can mark off your distance on a map as though you were walking cross-country. By the end of a year, you may find that you've walked a distance equal to that between San Francisco and San Diego—or between New York and Miami. This helps in setting long-term goals, too. For instance, you can promise yourself that by the end of the year, you'll have walked the same number of miles as you would had you walked from Chicago to Houston.

Step Three: Set a workout time. Have you ever noticed how easily you slip into routines? Perhaps you always brush your teeth before, not after, you shower in the morning; always put your left, not your right, shoe on first; or always take the same route to work every day. And have you ever noticed how you tend to feel you've forgotten to do something important if anything should interfere with one of these rituals? You may find it easy to stay with a walking program if you can allow it to become part of your daily routine—so much a part that you'll feel compelled to walk despite your own excuses for skipping a day. If you can get yourself into the habit of walking at a certain time every day, you'll accept it as part of your regular daily schedule and not just something to do during your "free time."

Many people feel they can't find the time in their busy schedules to exercise. But exercise, including walking, need not take much time, especially compared to the amount of time most Americans spend watching television. It's simply a matter of priorities. Others may feel so exhausted from work and their responsibilities at home that they feel they have no leftover energy with which to exercise. This can become a vicious cycle, though, because the more out of shape you are, the more easily you'll get tired out. To break the cycle, make time for walking and stick with it. You'll soon find you have more energy.

Step Four: Choose the best time of day to exercise. It's important to schedule your walking workouts for a time when you are least likely to have to cancel or interrupt them because of conflicting demands from work or home.

Some walkers like to venture out early in the morning, some even before daybreak. They like the solitude of early morning, when the streets are still empty of traffic and people. They can slowly get their minds and bodies going and do a little thinking in the silence. And if they are walking where they can see the horizon, they can savor the exhilarating sight of dawn.

Even some walkers who are decidedly not morning people—the types who ordinarily just drag themselves around till noon—swear by an early-morning walk. They say their morning walks give them a "jump start" on the day, making them feel more alert and energetic on the job. By the time they sit down at their desks, they feel invigorated enough to tackle any work that comes their way.

Lunch hours are an increasingly popular time for regular, vigorous walks. Some people walk for the first 45 minutes of their lunch hour and grab a bite during the last 15 minutes. Walking at lunchtime gets them out of the office (or house) and into a refreshing midday break. If you want to do your walking during your lunch hour, however, be sure you have enough time to accommodate the goals specified in your walking program.

Other walkers wait until they have left their work, putting their jobs behind them. A walk at this time of day provides a nice transition—a time to work off some of the day's tensions so that they aren't carried into family life.

Late evening seems to appeal to some people as the best time to work out. You might want to take a couple of factors into account, how-ever, before you set late evening as your walk-ing time. When you put walking as the last item on your agenda for the day, it often gets treated that way—last. You may tend to put other things in place of it or skip it because you don't have enough time or energy left. Also, some people find that a walk right before bedtime revs up their metabolism so much that they have difficulty falling asleep. On the other hand, some people find that a walk in the late evening can help them relax and unwind enough to fall asleep. So you may want to experiment with walking at this time before you decide to make it a habit.

Step Five: Dress the part. If possible, have a special outfit and wear it only for walking. How you look is not the point; it's how you feel. In changing from regular clothes into a "walking outfit," you can "psych yourself up" for the activity. In effect, you're telling yourself you mean business and really intend to collect all the rewards that are coming to you from walking. Be sure, however, that your outfit is appropriate for weather conditions.

Step Six: Think the part. What happens in your head is almost as important as what happens to your body. If you don't enjoy what you're doing, you'll begin to find reasons for not doing it.

Before you walk, try to get yourself into a positive, active frame of mind. As you walk, be aware of what's happening to your body. Feel your muscles work. Concentrate on the rhythmic flow of your movements. Walking can be a very pleasurable sensory experience.

Step Seven: Walk with others. If you're married, your spouse has to be on your side, says a study conducted at the Heart Disease and Stroke Control Program. The study followed men who were participating in an exercise program of one hour of physical activity three times a week for eight months. The men whose wives encouraged their participation had good attendance in the program; those men whose wives were neutral or had negative feelings about the exercise had a much poorer attendance record. The conclusion: The spouse's attitude was critical. So if you can, try encouraging your spouse or significant other to join you in your walking program or begin one of his or her own. You'll not only be increasing your chances of sticking with your program, you'll be encouraging your partner to increase his or her fitness and health, too.

Walking with a friend can also give you the advantage of companionship and encouragement. In a study conducted at the University of Toronto, scientists reported a greater dropout rate for individual exercise programs than for group programs. Only 47 percent of those in individual programs were still active at 28 weeks, compared with 82 percent of those in the group programs. If you think your motivation is weak—or weakening—walk with a partner or with several friends. (For more on using the "buddy system" in your walking routine, see Chapter 13).

Step Eight: Walk tall. Don't worry about what other people think. As you're walking down the street, you may think that everyone is looking at you. Chances are that no one is really paying any attention. And if somebody does stare, so what? You're doing something good for your body. Besides, they may simply be admiring your ambition.

SPICING UP
YOUR ROUTINE

The first step in establishing walking as a lifelong activity is to incorporate it into your everyday routine. Even if you have managed to build walking into your life, however, you may still need to add boredom-busting variations to your walking workouts to keep yourself from joining the all-too-ample ranks of the exercise dropouts. Variety is the spice of life. So whatever it takes to add variety to your walking routine, do it; it will help keep you committed to walking for a lifetime and make each walk more enjoyable than the last.

The novelty doesn't need to be as unusual as walking on stilts to do the trick (although some people do enjoy stilt-walking). You can try walking to music, walking with a friend or family member, taking a walking vacation, joining a walking club, participating in walking events, or adding other activities to your walking program. You may even want to try setting a walking record.

WALKING TO MUSIC

Walking to music is an excellent way to spice up your walking routine and keep up your momentum at the same time. Walking to music can also help you get your mind off pressures and problems so that you can concentrate on your walking program instead. Portable radios and tape players, handily equipped with headphones, make it possible for you to take your music with you as you walk.

A variety of audiotapes, specifically designed for walkers, is now available. These tapes feature music with a beat that closely matches the rhythm of a brisk walk. Some tapes are divided into three sequences: music for warming up, music for maintaining a heart rate fast enough to condition the heart and lungs, and music for cooling down. The beat helps you keep your pace, with the tempo starting out slowly, building gradually, then finally slowing down again. You can, of course, create your own tape using favorite tunes. Try to select music that has a clear beat to help you keep your walking rhythm.

Enjoy the music, but for the sake of safety, you still need to stay aware of your surroundings. It's a good idea to keep the volume control at a sensible level—not blasting—so you can hear any danger signals around you, such as honking car horns, shouting people, or barking dogs.

THE BUDDY SYSTEM

For many people, a daily, solitary walk is a welcome opportunity to be alone, to reflect on the events of the previous day or the day ahead. Walking, however, can also be a sociable activity. Even if you're breathing deeply, you can still chat with a walking companion. As a matter of fact, walking with a companion is a good way to take the "talk test" (see Chapter 4) to be sure you're not walking too fast. Moderate-paced walking shouldn't leave you breathless.

The hidden advantage of the "buddy system" is that it helps motivate you to walk. It's a whole lot harder to use an excuse not to walk, like "It's too cold out," or "I'm too busy today," when a friend is waiting for you. It's a reciprocal arrangement: Your buddy can help motivate you to walk when you are feeling lazy, and you can do the same thing when your buddy falls into a similar mood.

Even if you start out walking alone, you may find plenty of company—and potential walking partners—out there. These days, more and more people are rediscovering the joys of walking.

A FAMILY AFFAIR

One of the best ways to add fun to your walking routine is to make it a family affair. Like walking buddies, family members can boost your motivation—they may be even better at nudging your conscience to keep you in the swing of things when you'd just as soon take a day off or give up altogether.

One pleasant ritual you may want to introduce your family to is a relaxing evening amble in the twilight. Be sure to wait awhile after dinner, however, especially for a brisk walk. It's best to avoid strenuous exercise for at least two hours after eating.

If you're going to add variety to your own routine by making walking a family affair, be sure to bring the kids along. You may think, "I don't have to worry about the kids—they get lots of exercise." Although it is true that they probably do get more exercise than you, consider these questions: How much time do your children (or younger siblings, nieces, nephews, or grandchildren) spend watching television rather than riding their bikes or playing tag? While the kids may attend gym classes at school, are they really participating in aerobic activity? Do your children walk to school or do they get there by bus or car?

You may be bringing up your children to lead sedentary lives. Studies have shown that children mimic their parents' behavior, so if you've been sedentary, then in effect you may be teaching your children to be less active as well.

You also play an important role when it comes to your children's attitudes about television and automobiles. Most kids in the United States spend over four hours each day watching television. If your television is turned on most of the time, your children may learn passive leisure. They may grow up to be "couch potatoes." At some time during each day, you might want to assert yourself and turn off the television. While the set is off, encourage walking and other fun, physical activities.

As for your car, keep it in the garage and take it out only when trips really call for it. By relying less on your car, you will be teaching your children to build walking permanently into their lives. Some families that have tried this have become so wrapped up in walking that they now proclaim a "no-car day." On that day, no one can use the car except for an emergency.

In far too many schools, the emphasis is placed on athletics for the gifted few rather than for everyone. To compound the problem, physical education and athletics generally focus on team sports rather than on potentially lifelong activities such as walking. And what's even worse, burnout from participation in school athletics may even discourage future activity. How many times have you seen a coach discipline players by having them run laps or do push-ups as punishment for misbehavior or an error on the playing field? This punitive approach may actually discourage fitness.

In addition to adding variety to your routine, involving your children in your walking program is a great way to set an example for them and encourage them to develop and maintain physical fitness for the rest of their lives. Walking with your children also provides an opportunity for extra talking, sharing, and learning.

There's another advantage to walking as a family. Often, it's difficult for a family to pick an activity that everyone can participate in. Each family includes people of various ages, shapes, sizes, and levels of physical fitness. Not every family member will have the same skills in skiing, tennis, golf, or basketball. However, even toddlers can walk, and when they get tired, they can be placed in a stroller or baby sling.

Far too often, parents find themselves exasperated when they bring their young children along on a walk. There's no getting around it: If the children's legs are shorter, they will walk slower than you do. They may also want to use the walk as a time for adventure and looking about, which further slows down their pace. One solution is to allow more time for each walk, so you can let the children walk at their own pace—and enjoy yourself. If you have only a limited amount of time for a walk, you can push the child in a stroller or cart.

When walking with the family, make sure

to vary your route, even if you merely walk in the opposite direction every other day. You might also encourage the children to invite one or two of their friends along or have them walk the family dog. One more useful variation: Let one of the older children lead another child who shuts his or her eyes. This is an activity that is often used by educators to heighten a child's awareness of his or her surroundings and develop the nonvisual senses. Be sure, however, that you keep an eye on them as they do this. You might also try walking together to go out to dinner, to go shopping, or to go to religious services.

When walking along a road where there are no sidewalks, walk along the left side of the road, against the traffic. Teach children the rules of traffic, such as obeying traffic lights and crossing the street at crosswalks. And, as in driving, they need to learn to watch out for the other guy.

Finally, make sure the children wear light-colored clothing. If they are wearing dark clothing, have them wear bright arm bands or hats. That way, motorists can see them better.

Will you be able to talk your children into walking with you and staying in a walking program? Yes, provided you set an example yourself, and support your children with positive comments about their growing walking skills. In this way, you'll be able to maximize the health and happiness of your family's future generations.

Don't push your children into walking, however. Nagging won't do much good; you'll just turn them off of fitness. Try to encourage an atmosphere of cooperation and togetherness and a sense of adventure. Show them how much you enjoy your walks and they'll be more likely to follow your example.

WALKING VACATIONS

A walking vacation is a great way to add novelty to your walking program. Not only does a walking vacation give you something to plan for, it also gives you a lot to remember. Years after you enjoy a walking tour of Paris, for instance, the early-morning hustle and bustle you encounter as you walk through your own town may remind you of the sights, sounds, and smells of the city. Suddenly, you'll be transported back in time and place—all in the course of an ordinary stroll in your hometown.

Hiking trips are popular examples of walking vacations (see Chapter 7 for more on hiking). There's also an abundance of American cities to choose from, each with its unique parks and neighborhoods to explore. Foreign cities, towns, and countrysides also provide delightful territory for walking. Americans traveling abroad often remark on how much more hospitable other countries are to walking. Old World cities, built long before the automobile came to prominence, tend to offer meandering streets and broad, tree-lined boulevards that are ideal for walking.

Some countries also have walking traditions that can be a joy to discover on a walking vacation. One example is Switzerland, whose hills and mountains are criss-crossed with hiking trails. Often, the trails feature stations where the walker can take advantage of instructions and equipment for calisthenic exercises. Another lovely walking tradition is the evening promenade in Spain; whole families converge on central squares to stroll and greet one another.

Your walking tour can be as spartan or luxurious as you choose. You can arrange to spend your nights camping out in the wilderness or staying in hostels, inns, or hotels—and still spend your days walking. Unless you are an experienced hiker or long-distance walker, you'll want to limit most of your treks to about ten miles per day. If possible, arrange your travel plans so that you can take your time and walk at a comfortable pace.

It can take a lot of preparation to map out a walking tour. Some travel agencies offer pre-arranged walking tours, where your accommodations and your daily walking routes will be mapped out for you. Even if you go on a regular tour, you can try to skip the cabs and tour buses and walk to your destinations.

Carrying all the guidebooks, maps, and brochures you need to guide you in your walking vacations can be a weighty proposition. To relieve this burden, some enterprising companies are marketing walking tour guides on lightweight audiocassette tapes. Check with the tourist bureau at your destination, too. They may have prepared tour tapes that you can borrow, rent, or buy.

WALKING CLUBS

You may want to take a step beyond just walking with friends and family—and join a walking club. Clubs are springing up all over the country.

Many clubs sponsor walking events, which can put some zip into your walking program.

These events range from low-key togetherness walks to high-powered racewalking events. On the friendlier, noncompetitive end of the spectrum are 6- or 12-mile walking events called *volkswalks*—that's "people's walks" in German—sponsored by local branches of the American Volkssport Association.

Many worthy charities also sponsor walking events. (See Appendix B on page 235 for more information on walking events.) Remember, too, that many racewalkers—and freestyle walkers—join events that are meant primarily for joggers. Marathons are an example: Covering 26 miles is no mean feat, whether you jog, racewalk, or just plain walk the distance. Be sure that you prepare for these events, gradually increasing the distance of your daily walk.

CROSS-TRAINING

Cross-training means devoting oneself to more than one activity for fitness. By definition, it's a boredom buster, because you can switch from one activity to another. If you've been following a walking program, and you now feel that you're ready for a new challenge, a cross-training program may be for you.

For walkers, cross-training is an important opportunity to choose a companion activity that does what walking can't do—build upper body strength. Swimming, weight training, rowing, and cross-country skiing are all good companion activities.

You can devise your own personal cross-training routine, using walking as the cornerstone of your active lifestyle. Start by choosing just one new activity and do it on "off" days—the days when you don't do your fitness walking. Keep in mind that, just as in walking, you will need to progress with your companion activity gradually. After adding an activity on top of your regular walking routine, you'll want to wait at least three months before adding yet another activity.

"There's a promising future for cross-training," says James Rippe, M.D., an associate professor of medicine at Tufts University School of Medicine, who is both a walker and a jogger. "And walking is going to be one of those things that is increasingly used in cross-training." He notes that more and more top athletes—including runners and triathletes—are using brisk walking for their cross-training. The reason is that brisk walking and running use different muscles, so walking allows the athlete to work on strengthening various muscles and developing flexibility.

GOING FOR THE RECORD

The walkers who've earned a place in the record books, achieving amazing walking feats, provide an important source of inspiration for continuing your own walking program. Here are just a few inspiring examples from the annals of walking:

Robert Sweetgall completed a 11,208-mile solo walk and lecture tour that took him through 50 states in 50 weeks. Seven times during the walk, which was sponsored by the Rockport Company, he was flown back to the University of Massachusetts Medical Center, where Dr. Rippe and his colleagues conducted exhaustive medical tests on him. It became the most comprehensive scientific testing ever performed on the long-range effects of walking on an endurance athlete. The researchers found that Sweetgall's oxygen consumption rose during the walk. By the end, it was over 20 percent greater than that of the average man of his age, height, and weight.

Jesse Casteneda, a native of Mexico who lives in Albuquerque, New Mexico, continues to break walking records while raising funds for humanitarian causes. In 1973, he became the first person ever to walk over 300 miles (equivalent to the distance from Boston to Philadelphia) without stopping. He covered 302 miles in 102 hours and 59 minutes, with no breaks for sleeping— only the occasional break to use the bathroom in the trailer that came along to support him. In 1982, he walked across the country, from New York to California. He wasn't trying to break any record that time, but it took him a brief four-and-a-half months, averaging 35.2 miles a day, even with two days off per week spent meeting local people, visiting hospitals, and giving guest lectures. Before that, Casteneda broke the men's record for distance walked in 24 hours: He covered 142 miles and 448 yards.

Journalist **Steven Newman,** who lives in Ohio, completed the first documented solo walk around the earth. In his worldwalk, he walked more than 21,000 miles across 20 countries on five continents. The trip, which took 1,460 days, was achieved without any commercial sponsors or grants. Newman relied on the kindness of strangers the world over for sustenance.

David Kwan started out in Singapore on May 4, 1957, and walked all the way to London in 81 weeks. Kwan averaged 32 miles a day and passed through 14 countries during his 18,500-mile trek.

Plennie L. Wingo covered only 8,000 miles—a mere stroll compared to Kwan's long-distance achievement—but Wingo is in the record books. Why? Because Wingo walked backward the whole way. He wore special glasses that enabled him to see where he was going. Wingo started his journey in Santa Monica, California, on April 15, 1931; he arrived at his destination of Istanbul, Turkey, on October 24, 1932. Forty-five years later, at the age of 81, Wingo decided to celebrate the anniversary of his transcontinental backward walk by walking backward from Santa Monica, California, to San Francisco. He covered the 452 miles in 85 days.

CHAPTER 14

SHOES AND ACCESSORIES

We've said before that walking doesn't require much in the way of equipment. One of the only—and by far the most important—items that you'll need is a pair of sturdy, comfortable walking shoes. If you don't take time and care in selecting your walking shoes, you may be in for some serious discomfort.

In addition to walking shoes, there are a variety of accessories available that can increase your comfort, safety, and enjoyment as you walk. As you progress through your walking program, you may want to add them to your walking gear.

What to Look for in Shoes

As walking has gained popularity as a form of exercise, a wide variety of shoes meant specifically for walking has appeared on the market. The unique designs and features of many of these shoes have evolved from research into the mechanics of walking. This research has shown that the stresses put on the feet in walking are different from those exerted in other exercises such as jogging, tennis, and aerobics. If you walk, it makes good sense to select shoes designed specifically with walking in mind.

When you shop for walking shoes, keep in mind that the basic shape of the shoe should conform to the shape of your foot, and the toe box (the area around your toes) should be high enough, wide enough, and long enough to accommodate your toes comfortably. (See Chapter 9 for more on fitting walking shoes to prevent discomfort and injury.) But the fit isn't the only factor to consider.

You'll want to find shoes that cushion and support your feet as they hit the ground with each step. Shoe design, however, often involves a trade-off between cushioning and stability. A well-cushioned shoe may not control the foot's motion adequately. An extremely rigid shoe, on the other hand, may not provide the shock absorption and flexibility necessary for comfort.

If you have had stress fractures, joint problems, or back pain in the past, you may want to opt for a shoe that stresses cushioning over stability. You'll want a shoe that has a well-cushioned insole (the shock-absorbing lining inside the shoe upon which your foot rests) and midsole (the part of the sole between the insole and the very bottom of the shoe).

If, however, your foot tends to roll inward (pronate) as you walk, you may want to pick a pair of shoes that stresses stability. If you don't know whether you pronate or not, take a look at your other shoes. If the outer side of the heel and the inner side of the forefoot (under the big toe joint) show a great deal more wear than the rest of the sole, chances are that you pronate excessively. Most people pronate to some extent, but the more your feet tend to roll inward as they hit the ground, the more support you'll need to prevent foot problems. So look for a more rigid shoe with a sturdy heel counter (the cup at the back of the shoe that wraps around your heel). To test the heel counter of a shoe, try squeezing it. If it collapses, choose a different shoe.

To get the best of both worlds, look for a shoe with a midsole that contains two or three materials of different density (called dual or triple density). In these shoes, the softer, less dense materials cushion the feet while the firmer, denser materials stabilize the feet and make the shoes more durable. You may also want to try a shoe that has a heel cup (a padded, cup-like area inside the back of the shoe that cushions the heel and holds it in place).

The sole of the shoe should be flexible at the ball of the foot. If you can bend the shoe in the middle (below the arch support), however, you won't get enough arch support and your feet may tire easily.

The outsole (the very bottom of the sole that comes in contact with the ground) should be made of a durable, springy material like rubber yet should be soft enough so that if you press your fingernail into it, you can see a slight indentation. The outsole should also be patterned to provide traction.

Instead of the flat-bottomed sole found in running shoes, some walking shoes feature a distinct heel. This type of walking shoe may be a good choice for people who are prone to developing aching arches, midfoot pain *(plantar fasciitis),* and heel spurs (see Chapter 9). Some walking shoes have a "rocker" sole—that is, they are thicker under the ball of the foot than are other types of athletic shoes, and they curve upward in front. This design helps support the foot as the body's weight is transferred from the heel to the toe.

The uppers (the part of the shoe above the sole that covers the feet) should be made of soft material that "breathes," allowing sweat to evaporate. Leather, or a combination of leather and nylon, is a good choice. The uppers should have a padded heel collar (the part of the upper surrounding the opening of the shoe) and tongue. Some shoes feature a notched heel collar that helps prevent irritation of the Achilles tendon.

Your choice of uppers—and style—will rely, in part, on where and when you'll be doing most of your walking. If you walk to and from work, for instance, you may want to check out some of the new, dressier styles of walking shoes. If you'll be doing a lot of walking on uneven ground, such as on grass or gravel, you may want to look into high-topped walking shoes or hiking boots that offer greater stability and will protect your ankles.

When you shop for walking shoes, take your time. Examine each shoe carefully. Run your fingers along the inside of the upper to be sure there are no protruding seams that can cause blisters in the toe area. Poke your fingers into the insole and the heel area to be sure they're soft yet firm. When you try on a style, put both shoes on and lace them up. If you'll be wearing two pairs of socks when you walk, wear them when you try on your shoes. Be sure to walk around in the shoes—on both concrete and carpet.

Finally, remember to ask about the return policy on the shoes. Some stores will allow you to return or exchange shoes after a short trial period—as long as you haven't worn them outdoors.

RACEWALKING SHOES

Unlike fitness walking shoes, racewalking shoes can be harder to find—mainly because there are far fewer styles produced. Designed specifically for maximum speed in competitive racewalking, these shoes are very lightweight. Racewalking shoes have less cushioning in the sole and heel than do freestyle walking shoes, however, so unless you're a dedicated, competitive racewalker, stick with a fitness walking shoe. (For more information on racewalking, see Chapter 6.)

BOOTS FOR HIKING AND BACKPACKING

If you're going hiking—especially on rugged, uneven terrain—you'll need a pair of boots or shoes that protect and support your feet and ankles. Ideally, hiking boots should have high-top, padded collars that cover your ankles. The soles should be stiff—to protect the bottom of your feet from rocky terrain—and lugged or treaded—to provide good traction.

Another important feature is weight. If you're going on shorter walks, or if you'll be hiking through less rugged terrain, you may be able to get by with a pair of sturdy walking shoes. Or you might want to check out lightweight nylon hiking boots. They look more like athletic shoes, often weigh half as much as traditional hiking boots, and contain liners made of waterproof, breathable materials.

If you'll be doing a lot of hiking, through all kinds of weather, on rocky, uneven terrain, traditional hiking boots are probably your best bet. They're usually made of leather and have thick, heavy soles. They provide the best support and protection, but they're also heavier than the nylon models. (For more information on hiking, see Chapter 7.)

WALKING SOCKS

If you choose them wisely, socks can greatly increase foot comfort and help protect against foot problems as you walk. Good socks for walking need not be designed specifically for this activity. However, they should fit properly. Socks that are too small can cramp your toes and even increase the risk of foot problems. On the other hand, socks that are too large can bunch up, rub against your feet, and even cause blisters.

The socks you choose should be shaped to fit your feet and should be seamless, since friction can build up between a seam and the skin and promote blisters. They should also be thick enough to help absorb the forces that build up as the heel of the shoe strikes the ground. Often, this thickness is reinforced with a bit of extra padding where you need it most, at the heel and toe.

WALKING STICKS

Many walkers—especially those who also hike—like the feel of a walking stick. It helps them keep their rhythm as they walk. Using a walking stick can also increase the involvement of the upper body. On rough terrain, the stick can be used to detect holes, tree stumps, and unstable ground. It can also be used to ward off dogs.

Several different types of walking sticks are available. Some are made of lightweight aluminum. Others are solid and made of hard wood. The type of tip you'll want on the bottom of the walking stick will depend on the surface you're walking on. Pointy steel tips are useful for walking on icy surfaces and mountain trails. Plastic tips help keep wooden walking sticks from splintering when they're used on hard surfaces.

Some walking sticks can be broken down into two or three pieces for easy storage. Other models are made of reflective material and therefore serve as a safety device during evening walks. Some walking sticks even have tips that unscrew to reveal handy items like a compass or a sundial. Of course, if you live near a wooded area, you may simply want to choose a sturdy, fallen branch and use it as a homemade walking stick.

PEDOMETERS

A pedometer is a device that gives an estimate of the distance you travel on foot. It registers the number of steps you take by sensing the body's movements. Most pedometers need to be calibrated—in other words, you have to punch in the length of your stride first. One way to do this is to mark off a 100-foot stretch of level ground. Then as you walk that stretch, count the number of strides you take. When you've reached the end of the marked distance, divide 100 by the number of strides you took and enter the resulting stride length into the pedometer. If you enjoy jogging as well as walking, however, be aware that you can't use the same pedometer—set to the same adjustment—to gauge your performance in both activities. (That's because your jogging stride will be longer than your walking stride.) Instead, you'll either have to get two pedometers—one for walking and the other for jogging—or you'll need to keep adjusting the same pedometer back and forth for the two activities.

Some pedometers attach to your waistband, while others are placed around the wrist or built into shoes. Some devices can also estimate your average speed, the number of calories you burn, and the amount of time it takes you to walk a certain distance.

PULSE MONITORS

Several types of devices are available to measure your pulse as you walk. Some are hand-held. Others are worn on the wrist like a watch. There are also pulse monitors that strap around the chest and measure the electrical impulses of the heart, much like an electrocardiogram. Pulse gauges offer an advantage over manual pulse-taking because they allow you to find out your heart rate while you walk, instead of having to stop to count heartbeats. (Remember, your heart rate begins to slow down within 15 seconds of when you stop walking.) Some very elaborate pulse monitors are available that use ultrasound technology to measure the heart rate.

PORTABLE RADIOS AND TAPE PLAYERS

Lightweight, portable radios, tape players, and compact disc players are popular walking companions. They come in a variety of sizes and styles, from those that attach to your belt to those that are incorporated into headsets. Some headphones are even built into earmuffs—a handy innovation in the winter.

Remember, for the sake of safety, it's a good idea to keep the volume control at a sensible level. If you're blasting the music, you may not hear danger signals around you, such as approaching cars or barking dogs.

CARRYING VALUABLES

Even if you're not going on a day-long hike, you may still need to carry a few things—money, keys, identification—as you walk. One popular way to do so is to use a "fanny pack." A fanny pack is a specially made belt with a zippered pouch. The belt can be adjusted so that the pouch area rests in front or in back—whichever is most comfortable. (If you will be walking in a crowded area, you'll probably want the pouch facing forward for safety's sake.) Some manufacturers even make socks and shoes that come with tiny, sealable pouches for keys, change, and identification.

Special packs are also available for carrying infants while you walk. These packs feature a collar to support the baby's head, as well as an inner pouch to position the infant securely. Newborns, who need more support, are more secure when carried on the chest. The same pack can later be adjusted to carry the older infant on your back.

WATER BOTTLES

From Army-style canteens to high-tech insulated thermoses, a variety of portable containers are on the market for carrying liquids during walks. Some models feature an insulated carrier that keeps the contents of the bottle cool on hot days and warm on cold days. Others have a dual function. They come equipped with a handle so that you can use the filled container as a hand-held weight.

REFLECTIVE GEAR

Reflective gear is important for your safety when you walk at night, particularly if you are walking along a road in an area with no streetlights or sidewalks. When a car's lights hit the reflective gear, you become visible at a much greater distance than you would be if you wore nonreflective white or light-colored garments. Reflective gear does not guarantee safety, however, so you'll still need to stay alert and face the traffic as you walk.

Reflective material is incorporated into many garments, including vests, headbands, belts, sashes, and leg bands. You can also purchase reflective safety trim that can be sewn, taped, or ironed onto your walking outfit. Ideally, the reflective gear should be worn on the chest, arms, waist, legs, and ankles. It's especially important to wear reflective material on your legs and ankles, because much of the light from headlights is directed toward the ground. And because these body parts are moving, they are more likely to attract the driver's attention. (For more information on walking at night, see Chapter 11 and Appendix C.)

<u>WALKING CLUBS</u>

WALKING CLUBS AND ORGANIZATIONS

American Volkssport Association
1001 Pat Booker Road, Suite 101
Universal City, TX 78148
(210) 659–2112

North American Racewalking Foundation
P.O. Box 50312
Pasadena, CA 91115–0312
(818) 577–2264

USA Track & Field
(national governing body for racewalking)
P.O. Box 120
Indianapolis, IN 46206–0120
(317) 261–0500

Walkabout International
835 Fifth Avenue
Room 407
San Diego, CA 92101
(619) 231–SHOE

HIKING CLUBS AND ORGANIZATIONS

American Youth Hostels
Travel Department
P.O. Box 37613
Washington, DC 20013–7613
(202) 783–6161

Appalachian Mountain Club
5 Joy Street
Boston, MA 02108
(617) 523–0636

Appalachian Trail Conference
P.O. Box 807
Harper's Ferry, WV 25425
(304) 535–6331

Family Campers and RVers
4804 Transit Road, Building 2
Depew, NY 14043
(716) 668–6242

Florida Trail Association
P.O. Box 13708
Gainesville, FL 32604
(904) 378–8823

Long-Distance Hikers' Association
Cindy Ross (coordinator)
Box 194, RD 2
Kempton, PA 19529
(610) 756–6995

Sierra Club
85 Second Street
2nd Floor
San Francisco, CA 94105
(415) 977–5500

U.S. Orienteering Federation
P.O. Box 1444
Forest Park, GA 30051
(404) 363–2110

WALKING Magazine
9–11 Harcourt Street
Boston, MA 02116
(617) 266–3322

Wilderness Society
900 17th Street NW
3rd Floor
Washington, DC 20006
(202) 833–2300

Yellowstone Association
P.O. Box 168
Yellowstone National Park, WY 82190
(307) 344–7381

NATIONAL PARK SERVICE

For information on National Park
Service facilities for hiking and
camping, contact:

Public Affairs
National Park Service
Department of the Interior, Room 3043
Washington, DC 20240
(202) 208–3100

WALKING EVENTS

Interested in strutting your stuff? The events below will appeal to all types of walkers. Call or write the organizations below for more information.

Appalachian Long Distance Association Annual Gathering

Long-Distance Hikers' Association
Cindy Ross (coordinator)
Box 194, RD 2
Kempton, PA 19529
(215) 756–6995

Volkssport Reunion Walk

American Volkssport Association
1001 Pat Booker Road, Suite 101
Universal City, TX 78148
(210) 659–2112

Walkabout International 56-mile One-Day Endurance Walk

Walkabout International
835 Fifth Avenue, Room 407
San Diego, CA 92101
(619) 231–SHOE

WalkAmerica

March of Dimes
To raise funds to prevent birth defects, contact your local March of Dimes chapter or March of Dimes Headquarters.
1275 Mamaroneck Avenue
White Plains, NY 10605
(914) 428–7100

Walk with Your Doc

American Diabetes Association
To raise funds for the American Diabetes Association,
contact your local American Diabetes Association chapter.

CHECKLISTS AND REMINDERS

TAKING YOUR PULSE

There are two main locations for checking your pulse—the carotid artery in your neck (just to the side of your throat) and the radial artery in your wrist (on the inner side of your wrist, below the heel of your hand).

Use the index and middle fingers of one hand to detect your pulse.

When you've found your pulse, count the number of beats for ten seconds. Then multiply that number by six to determine your heart rate.

You can also try counting your pulse for six seconds and multiplying by ten. Counting for six seconds is especially useful when you're taking your pulse during a walk, because there's less of a chance that your heart rate will slow down before you've gotten an accurate count.

FINDING YOUR TARGET
HEART RATE RANGE

(Using Your Maximum Heart Rate Reserve)

Step One: Measure your resting heart rate by counting your pulse for ten seconds and multiplying by six. (Do this at rest.)

Step Two: Subtract your resting heart rate from your maximum heart rate. (You can find your maximum heart rate by taking an exercise test or by subtracting your age from 220.)

Step Three: Multiply the result of Step Two by .4 (40 percent) and add that to the result of Step One to find the lower limit of your maximum heart rate reserve target zone.

Step Four: Multiply the result of Step Two by .85 (85 percent) and add that to the result of Step One to find the upper limit of your maximum heart rate reserve target zone.

HOT WEATHER CHECKLIST

❑ Drink plenty of cold water before, during, and after walks.

❑ Wear as little clothing as possible.

❑ Choose loose-fitting clothing made of lightweight, breathable fabric. Cotton is a wise choice because it absorbs perspiration and promotes evaporation of sweat. Spread petroleum jelly on areas prone to chafing. Shun walking outfits made of rubber, plastic, or other nonporous materials.

❑ Choose light-colored clothing to reflect the sun's rays.

❑ Cover your head with a lightweight, light-colored cap. Try soaking it in cold water before putting it on your head.

❑ Wear a waterproof sunscreen with a Sun Protection Factor (SPF) of 15 or more.

❑ Slow down your pace and decrease the intensity of your walk when humidity is high. Walk in a shaded area such as a park or forest preserve.

❑ Avoid walking in late morning or early afternoon when the sun's rays are strongest; instead, walk in the evening or early morning.

Recognizing Heat Injury

No matter how fit you are, you need to be careful when you walk in hot weather—especially if the humidity is high. Even experienced athletes can fall victim to serious heat-related ailments if they don't take special precautions. Remember, overexposure to heat can produce a range of effects—from a simple skin rash to potentially deadly heatstroke.

Heat cramps

Symptoms of heat cramps are painful muscle spasms, usually in the legs or abdomen, that occur during or after intense exercise. Body temperature is normal or near normal.

The victim of heat cramps should move to a cool area, rest, and sip cold water. The affected muscle should be massaged gently to relieve cramps.

Heat exhaustion

Symptoms of heat exhaustion include weakness; dizziness; collapse; headache; weak, rapid pulse; cold, clammy, pale skin; heavy sweating; dilated pupils; and normal, or near-normal body temperature.

The victim of heat exhaustion should lay down in a cool area and sip cold water. The victim's clothing should be loosened.

Heatstroke

Heatstroke is a medical emergency. Immediate steps to cool the victim must be taken to avoid a fatal outcome.

Symptoms of heatstroke include hot, dry skin; lack of sweating; rapid pulse; abdominal cramps; headache; dizziness; delirium; loss of consciousness; and high body temperature.

The victim should be moved to a cool area and placed in an icewater bath or covered with ice packs until emergency medical treatment is available.

COLD WEATHER CHECKLIST

When the snow starts to fall and the temperature drops, it's easy to slip into inactivity. But even in the winter you must keep up your walking program to maintain your fitness level. (Getting out of the house can also make you feel better and help fight the winter blues.) Be sure you've prepared yourself for low temperatures, however. Before you step out the door, be sure to review the following checklist.

❑ Wear dark-colored clothing to absorb the sun's rays.

❑ Dress in warm, loose-fitting layers to trap body heat and keep cold air out.

❑ If you're male, wear an extra pair of shorts to keep the groin area warm.

❑ Top off your layers of clothing with a breathable, waterproof windbreaker.

❑ Unzip or remove outermost layers as you begin to heat up.

❑ Wear a warm hat that covers your ears or wear earmuffs in addition to a hat.

❑ In cold, windy weather, cover all exposed skin to avoid frostbite. A ski mask or scarf can be used to protect the face.

❑ Wear mittens instead of gloves—or wear mittens on top of gloves—to trap heat around fingers.

❑ Wear calf- or knee-length socks made of an absorbent material.

❑ Wear a waterproof sunscreen on all exposed skin.

❑ Drink plenty of water before, during, and after your walks to avoid dehydration. Do not drink alcoholic beverages before or during your walks.

❑ Review the Windchill Index chart in Chapter 10 so you'll know when to move your walking program indoors.

Recognizing Cold Injury

Frostbite

Signs of frostbite include pain, numbness, and eventual loss of function in the affected area. Frostbitten skin often appears white or blue.

The victim of frostbite should be moved to a warm place. The frostbitten area should be re-warmed gradually and carefully by soaking it in lukewarm—not hot—water. Frostbitten skin should not be massaged or rubbed (especially not with snow). Avoid placing the frostbitten area in or near intense heat, as this may burn the numb skin.

Hypothermia

Symptoms of hypothermia include severe shivering, slurred speech, and difficulty in walking. If body temperature drops below 90 degrees Fahrenheit, shivering may cease and the victim may appear confused or may lapse into unconsciousness. Eventually, cardiac arrest and death can occur if emergency measures aren't taken.

The victim of hypothermia should be moved to a warm area and covered with blankets until medical treatment is available. Warm, nonalcoholic beverages should be given to victims that are conscious. Do not rub the victim's hands or feet.

NIGHTTIME WALKING CHECKLIST

❑ Walk on sidewalks whenever possible.

❑ If you must walk in the street, walk on the left side of the road, facing traffic. Use extra caution when approaching intersections.

❑ Wear light-colored or white clothing.

❑ Wear reflective trim that can be sewn, taped, or ironed onto your walking outfit. Be sure to wear some on your legs and ankles, since they will be moving and may be more likely to catch a motorist's attention.

❑ Carry a flashlight and keep it lighted as you walk to alert motorists of your presence.

❑ Avoid walking on an unfamiliar road or path at night. Check out the road during daylight hours first so you'll be aware of any dangers, including dogs, curves, ditches, or potholes.

❑ Don't look directly at the headlights of on-coming vehicles. Instead, look off to the side and use your peripheral (side) vision to detect vehicles.

❑ If a car seems to be bearing down on you, stop walking and step off the road.

FOOD GUIDE PYRAMID

One easy way to keep track of what you're eating and improve your food choices is to refer to the Food Guide Pyramid. The accompanying chart illustrates the Food Guide Pyramid and provides suggestions for choosing the healthiest foods from each group.

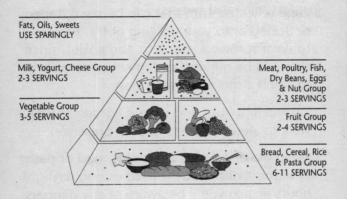

Fats, Oils, Sweets
USE SPARINGLY

Milk, Yogurt, Cheese Group
2-3 SERVINGS

Meat, Poultry, Fish,
Dry Beans, Eggs
& Nut Group
2-3 SERVINGS

Vegetable Group
3-5 SERVINGS

Fruit Group
2-4 SERVINGS

Bread, Cereal, Rice
& Pasta Group
6-11 SERVINGS

The top part of the pyramid shows fats, oils, and sweets. Salad dressings, cream, butter, margarine, sugars, soft drinks, candies, sweet desserts, and alcoholic beverages are found in this group. These foods provide calories but few vitamins and minerals.

You'll notice that some fat or sugar symbols are shown in the pyramid's other food groups as well. According to the U.S. Department of Agriculture, that's to remind you that some foods in these groups can also be high in fat and added sugars, such as cheese or ice cream from the milk group or french fries from the vegetable group. When choosing foods for a healthful diet, remember to consider the fat and added sugars of all the food groups, not just fats, oils, and sweets.

EATING WELL

Remember, you don't have to starve yourself or give up all of your favorite foods in order to improve your eating habits and control your weight. The following recommendations from the American Heart Association offer ideas on how to make gradual changes in your cooking and eating habits:

○ Eat a variety of foods from the various food groups to help you get all the nutrients you need and to keep mealtime from becoming a bore. (See the Food Pyramid on page 58 for more information on the various food groups.)

○ Choose lean cuts of meat and trim away any visible fat.

○ Limit the amount of lean meat, fish, and poultry you eat to no more than six ounces a day.

○ Substitute vegetable proteins such as dried beans, peas, or legumes for meat proteins as often as you can.

○ Choose fish, poultry, and veal more often than beef, lamb, or pork.

○ Trim the skin off of poultry before eating.

○ Substitute skim milk and low-fat cheeses for whole milk products.

○ Try substituting two egg whites for one whole egg in recipes.

○ Avoid frying foods. Instead, use cooking methods that help remove fat, such as baking, boiling, broiling, roasting, or stewing.

INDEX

A

Abdominal muscles
  back pain and, 134–135
  strengthening exercises for, 113
  walking for toning, 21
Accessories
  for hiking, 98–101
  for walking, 179, 224–230
Acclimatization to heat, 143–144
Achilles tendon
  injuries to, 126–128, 221
  stretching exercise for, 109
Aerobic exercise
  definition of, 22
  examples of, 22, 36
  health and, 25, 32–33, 35–36
Aging
  exercise and, 28–29, 55
  injury prevention and, 28–29
  walking and, 28–29
American Heart Association
  dietary recommendations, 58–59, 247–248
  exercise recommendations, 35–36
Anaerobic exercise, 23
Angina pectoris, 34, 138–139
  cold weather and, 162–163
Ankles, injuries to/pain in, 83, 126–128, 132, 221
Apparent temperature, 149–151
Appetite, exercise and, 15
Arch support, 127, 220
Arm muscles, walking for toning, 21, 82
Arthritis
  aging and, 55
  benefits of exercise for, 6, 31
Asthma, exercise and, 54, 163

Attitude, for walking success, 192–200

B

Back pain, 133–135
Basic Starter Program, 8–9, 73–75
Basic Walking Program, 9, 76–80
Blisters, 123–125, 159, 224
Blood pressure. *See* High blood pressure.
Borg scale, 66
Breathing techniques
  basic guidelines, 71
  for side stitch prevention, 136
  for stress management, 48
Bunions, 121–122

C

Calf muscles
  soreness of, 133
  stretching exercise for, 108
  walking for toning, 20
Calluses, 125
Calories, weight loss/control and, 13, 15, 16, 17–18, 78
Camping, 100–101, 103
Carbohydrates, dietary, 56, 60
Carotid artery, taking pulse at, 63, 237
Chest pain, 34, 136–140, 162–163
  angina pectoris, 34, 138–139, 162–163
  cold weather and, 162–163
  heart attack symptoms, 139
  heartburn, 138
  heart disease and, 34, 137, 138–140, 162–163
  muscular causes, 137–138
Cholesterol, blood levels of
  exercise and, 35, 83

Cholesterol, blood levels of
(continued)
  heart disease and, 35,
    36–37
Cholesterol, dietary, 56–57
Chronic fatigue, 43–44
Clothing
  for cold–weather walking,
    97, 156–157, 158–160,
    161, 242
  for foggy weather, 166
  for hiking, 96–98, 102
  for hot–weather walking,
    147–148, 239
  for nighttime walking, 156,
    181, 229–230, 245
  rain gear, 97, 164
Cold weather, walking in,
    151–164, 242–244
  clothing for, 97, 156–157,
    158–160, 161, 242
  cold injury, 152–154, 158,
    159, 244
  cramps and, 131
  footwear for, 158, 165
  health problems and,
    162–164
  snow, 164–165
  windchill factor, 152,
    155–156
Cooldown
  basic guidelines, 107
  from freestyle walking,
    72–73
  soreness and, 133
Corns, 120, 159
Corporate fitness programs,
    190–191
Cramps, muscle, 131–132,
    137, 144
Cross-training, 212–213

D

Depression, 6, 47, 49–51
Diabetes, 39, 54–55

Diet. See also Water intake.
  basic guidelines, 55–61,
    246–248
  heart disease and, 35,
    36–37, 57
  meals to eat before exercise,
    60
  osteoporosis and, 41
  for weight loss and control,
    12–13, 15–16
Dietary Guidelines for
    Americans, 56
Dieting, 12–13

E

Electrocardiograms, 53, 140
Emphysema, 76
Endorphins, 51
Energy level
  benefits of walking for, 6,
    43–44
  overexertion and, 68
Events, walking, 212, 235–236
Exercise
  aerobic capacity and, 26
  American Heart Association
    recommendations for,
    35–36
  dropout rates, 12, 24,
    183–185
  health benefits summarized,
    30–33. See also Health
    benefits of exercise.
  after meals, 59–60
  meals as energy source for,
    60
  Surgeon General's
    recommendations for, 30,
    32–33
Exercises for flexibility. See
    Stretches.
Exercises for strength, 108,
    111–116
  basic guidelines, 108
  importance of, 118

Exercises for strength
(continued)
  for injury prevention,
    129–130, 131, 135
  instructions for, 111–116
    Abdominal Curls, 113
    Bent-Over Row, 115
    Flies, 114
    Lateral Raises, 116
    Push-ups, 111–112
    shin splint prevention
      exercise, 129–130
Exercise tests, 53–54, 62

F

Fat, body
  cancer and, 40
  healthy percentage of, 18
  measuring, 18–19
  racewalking and, 83
  weight loss/control and, 12,
    13, 18
Fat, dietary
  consumption guidelines,
    56–57, 58, 59
  heart disease and, 35, 36–37
Fatigue
  chronic, benefits of exercise
    for, 43–44
  overexertion and, 68
Feet, injuries to/pain in,
  119–126, 158, 159, 220,
  224
First aid
  Achilles tendonitis, 128
  blisters, 124–125
  cold injury, 152–154, 244
  frostbite, 152–153, 244
  heat injury, 145–146, 240,
    241
  hypothermia, 153–154, 244
  ingrown toenails, 121
  muscle cramps and spasms,
    131–132
  muscle soreness, 133

First aid *(continued)*
  neuromas, 123
  RICE (rest, ice, compression,
    and elevation technique),
    128
  side stitch, 136
  for sprains, 132
  for walker's heel, 126
First aid kit, 99
Flexibility
  cross-training for, 213
  walking and, 105–106
  See also Stretches.
Food Guide Pyramid, 57–58,
  246–247
Form (style)
  for freestyle walking, 70–72
  for racewalking, 84–90
Fractures, metatarsal stress,
  123
Freestyle walking, 69–80
  Basic Starter Program, 8–9,
    73–75
  Basic Walking Program, 9,
    76–80
  competitions, 212
  cool-down after, 72–73
  health considerations, 80
  how to get started, 73
  Special Starter Program, 8–9,
    75–76
  style of walking for, 70–72
  warm-up for, 72–73
Frostbite
  causes and symptoms, 152,
    244
  prevention, 158, 159, 242
  treatment, 152–153, 244

G

Gluteal muscles, back pain
  and, 135
Guidelines for Fitness in
  Healthy Adults, 64–65

H

Hammertoes, 122
Hamstring muscles
  back pain and, 135
  stretching exercise for, 110
  walking for toning, 21
Health benefits of exercise,
    30–41. *See also* Mental
    health benefits of exercise.
  arthritis, 6, 31
  cancer, 40
  diabetes, 39
  digestion, 6, 40
  heart disease risk, 6, 25,
    33–37
  high blood pressure, 37,
    38–39
  osteoporosis, 6, 31, 41
  quality of life, 41
  summary of, 30–33
Health clubs, 174, 178
Health considerations
  cold-weather walking and,
    162–164
  with freestyle walking
    programs, 80
  physical examinations,
    52–54
Heart, walking for
    conditioning of, 23
Heart attack
  exercise and, 25, 34–35,
    80
  symptoms of, 139–140
Heartburn, 138
Heart disease
  chest pain with, 34, 137,
    138–140, 162–163
  cold-weather walking and,
    162–163
  diet and, 35, 36–37, 57
  exercise for reducing risk of,
    6, 25, 33–37
  mortality rate, 33

Heart disease *(continued)*
  pre-exercise testing for,
    53–54
Heart rate, 61–67
  for Basic Starter Program, 74
  for Basic Walking Program,
    76–77
  calculating maximum, 62
  pulse monitors for
    measuring, 226–227
  for Special Starter Program,
    76
  taking pulse for measuring,
    63, 65–66, 237
Heat cramps, 144, 149, 151,
    240
Heat exhaustion, 144–145,
    149, 151, 240
Heat Index, 149–151
Heatstroke, 145–146, 151, 241
Heel, injuries to/pain in,
    125–126, 220, 224
Heel spurs, 125–126, 220
High blood pressure, 37–39
  cold weather and, 163
  exercise and, 37, 38–39
  gender and, 37
  heart disease and, 36
Hiking, 93–104
  calories burned by, 17
  clothing for, 96–98, 102
  clubs and organizations, 94,
    232–233
  conditioning for, 95–96
  equipment for, 98–101
  footwear for, 97, 223
  locations for, 93–95,
    103–104
  safety for, 99, 101–103
  on vacations, 209, 210–211
Hip flexor muscles, walking for
    toning, 21
Hip injuries, 28, 83
Hot weather, walking in,
    142–151, 239–241

Hot weather, walking in
    (continued)
  clothing for, 147–148, 239
  Heat Index, 149–151
  heat injury, 144–146, 149,
    151, 240–241
Humidity, 143, 149–151, 239
Hypertension. *See* High blood
    pressure.
Hypothermia, 152, 153–154,
    244

I

Inactivity
  among children, 205
  heart disease and, 35–36
  obesity and, 14
  osteoporosis and, 41
Indoor walking, 172–178
Ingrown toenails, 121
Injuries. *See also* First aid.
  to Achilles tendon, 126–128,
    221
  to ankles and legs, 83,
    126–133, 221
  downhill walking and, 170
  to feet, 119–126, 158, 159,
    220, 224
  flexibility and, 106, 118
  to hip joints, 28, 83
  to knees, 83, 88, 130–131
  pregnancy and, 26
  racewalking and, 83
  steps for preventing, 118
  to toes, 119–123, 224
  walking for preventing, 28–29
  walking vs. other exercise
    and, 7, 24, 27–28
Ischemia, cardiac, 34

J

Jogging
  aerobic capacity and, 23, 24,
    25
  calories burned by, 17, 82
  injuries from, 27–28

K

Knees, injuries to/pain in, 83,
    88, 130–131

L

Lower body strength, 19–22,
    169
Lungs, walking for
    conditioning of, 23
Lupus, cold weather and, 164

M

Mall walking, 172–174
Marathons, 91, 212
Mask, for filtering air, 179
Massage
  for muscle soreness, 133
  for stress reduction, 48–49
Maximum heart rate,
    calculating, 62
Maximum heart rate reserve,
    25, 63–64, 238
  for Basic Starter Program, 74
  for Basic Walking Program, 77
Mental health benefits of
    exercise, 42–51
  alertness, 44
  depression, 6, 49–51
  energy level, 6, 43–44
  sleep, 44–45
  stress, 6, 45–49
Metabolic rate
  exercise-related alertness
    and, 44
  weight loss/control and, 13,
    14–15, 18
Metatarsal stress fractures, 123
Mineral supplements, 60
Motivation, 185, 192–200,
    201–216
Muscles. *See also* Exercises for
    strength; Strength.
  cramps and spasms,
    131–132, 137, 144
  imbalance of, 129–130

Muscles *(continued)*
  relaxation techniques, 48–49
  soreness and stiffness, 91,
    132–133, 170
  toned in walking, 6, 19–22,
    169
  wasting due to dieting, 12, 14

N

Neuromas, 122–123
Night, walking at, 181,
    229–230, 245
Nutrition. *See* Diet; Food.

O

Obesity, 14, 31. *See also*
    Weight loss and control.
Orthotics, 122, 131
Osteoporosis
  aging and, 29, 40–41, 55
  benefits of exercise for, 6,
    31, 41

P

Pain. *See also* First aid; Injuries.
  ankles and legs, 126–133, 221
  back, 133–135
  chest, 136–140, 162–163
  feet, 119–126, 158, 159,
    220, 224
  importance of paying
    attention to, 68,
    117–118, 139
  knees, 83, 88, 130–131
  muscle cramps, spasms and
    soreness, 91, 131–133, 170
  side stitch, 135–136
  toes, 119–123
  when to contact physician,
    68, 118, 139
Parks, hiking and walking in
    city parks, 170
  national and state parks,
    94–95, 234
Physical examinations, 52–54
Plantar fasciitis, 125, 220

Posture
  back pain and, 134
  for freestyle walking, 70
  pregnancy and, 27
  for racewalking, 89
Pregnancy, walking during,
    26–27
Progress, recording of, 51,
    194–195
Protein, dietary, 56, 60
Pulse. *See also* Heart rate.
  cautions for taking during
    exercise, 65–66
  how to take, 63, 237
Pulse monitors, 226–227

Q

Quadriceps muscles
  stretching exercise for, 109
  walking for toning, 21, 22

R

Racewalking, 81–92
  benefits of, 82–83
  calories burned by, 17, 82
  competitions, 83, 91–92, 212
  form for, 84–90
  injury prevention with, 83
  organizations, 231
  rules for, 84–85
  shoes for, 222
  warm-up for, 90–91
Radial artery, taking pulse at,
    63, 237
Rating of perceived exertion
    (RPE), 66–67
Raynaud's disease, and cold-
    weather walking, 163–164
Recording progress, 51,
    194–195
Records set by walkers,
    214–216
Relaxation, of muscles, 48–49
RICE (rest, ice, compression,
    and elevation), 128

RPE (rating of perceived
  exertion), 66–67
Runner's knee, 88, 130–131

S

SAD (seasonal affective
  disorder), 151
Safety, 178–181
  for children, 208
  for hiking, 99, 101–103
  at night, 181, 229–230, 245
  with traffic, 178–179,
    180–181, 208, 227,
    229–230, 245
Schedules, for walking, 79,
    195–198
  during hot weather, 146,
    239
Scleroderma, cold weather
  and, 163–164
Seasonal affective disorder
  (SAD), 151
Shin splints, 128–130
Shoes, 217–223
  care of, 124
  for cold-weather walking,
    158, 165
  cushioning from, 127,
    218–219, 220
  for hiking, 97, 223
  leg pain and, 127, 129
  proper fit for walking,
    119–120, 121, 218
  for racewalking, 222
  support from, 127, 218–219
Side stitch, 135–136
Soreness, muscle, 91,
    132–133, 170
Special Starter Program, 8–9,
    75–76
Sprains, 132
Stairs, walking on, 79,
    169–170, 186–187
Starter Programs, 8–9, 73–76
Stiffness, muscle, 132–133

Strength
  cross-training and, 213
  walking for lower body,
    19–22, 169
Stress
  cholesterol levels and, 35
  massage for managing,
    48–49
  obesity and, 14
  physiology of, 46–47
  symptoms of, 47
  walking for managing, 6,
    45–49
Stress fractures, metatarsal,
    123
Stretches
  basic guidelines, 107, 108
  guidelines for racewalking,
    90–91
  importance of, 22, 72, 118
  Standing Achilles Stretch, 109
  Standing Calf Stretch, 108
  Standing Chest Stretch, 110
  Standing Hamstrings Stretch,
    110
  Standing Quadriceps Stretch,
    109
Stride length, for freestyle
  walking, 71
Stroke, 25, 34
Style. *See* Form.
Sun protection
  clothing for, 147, 148, 239
  in cold weather, 160–161,
    242–243
Sunstroke (heatstroke),
    145–146, 151, 241
Surgeon General's report, 30,
    32–33

T

"Talk test," 67–68, 203
Target heart rate range,
    62–67, 238
  for Basic Starter Program, 74

Target heart rate range
   (continued)
   for Basic Walking Program,
      76–77, 78
   calculating, 63–64, 238
   for Special Starter Program,
      76
   for weight loss, 78
Tendonitis, of Achilles tendon,
   126–127
Thirst reflex, 158
Tick bites, 102–103
Time, for walking, 182–200
   finding, 79, 185–192
   during hot weather, 146, 239
   scheduling, 79, 195–198
   during working hours,
      186–188, 190–192, 197
Toenails, ingrown, 121
Toes, injuries to/pain in,
   119–123, 224
Toning, of muscles, 6, 19–22,
   169. See also Exercises for
   strength; Strength.
Trails, hiking, 103–104, 210
Treadmills, walking on,
   175–178

U

Upper body strength
   exercise for building, 22,
      111–112, 114–116
   racewalking and, 82
   walking and, 21, 106–107

V

Vacations, walking during,
   209–211
Vitamin supplements, 60

W

Walker's heel, 125–126
Walking tours, 209–211

Warm-up. See also Stretches.
   basic guidelines, 107
   for freestyle walking, 72–73
   for racewalking, 90–91
Water intake
   basic guidelines, 60–61
   in cold weather, 158, 243
   cramps and, 131
   for hikers, 98, 101–102
   in hot weather, 60–61, 143,
      145, 146, 239
Weather conditions, 141–166,
   239–244
   for hiking, 96–98
   indoor walking for avoiding,
      173, 174
   miscellaneous weather
      conditions, 164–166
   rain, 97, 164, 165
Weight loss and control, 6,
   12–19
   balancing calories and
      activity for, 13, 14–15, 16,
      78
   Basic Walking Program for, 78
   dietary changes for, 12–13,
      15–16, 57
   goal setting for, 193
   metabolic rate and, 13, 15, 18
   uphill and stair walking for,
      17–18, 169
Weights, walking with, 24
Weight training, 22, 106–107,
   114–116
Wind, walking in, 165
Windchill factor, 152, 155–156
Windchill index, 155